GROWL AND PROWL

DOMINICK

NYT AND USA TODAY BESTSELLING AUTHOR

EVE LANGLAIS

PROLOGUE

"Terminate him." The cold command jolted the doctor.

"You can't be serious." Johan shoved at his glasses, already firmly seated on his nose. He couldn't help but fidget.

"I am very serious. He's useless to me," said the man financing the project.

Known simply as Mr. X, no one knew his actual name, but everyone feared him. Always dressed in a suit with oversized, wraparound sunglasses, Mr. X tended to appear abruptly and make sweeping changes with a barked command.

Dr. Johan Philips stood beside his employer as they observed the subject in question through the one-way glass that looked upon a room twenty feet below. Set up as a gym, it had cushioned mats, bars, and ropes to

EVE LANGLAIS

climb. At any time of day, at least two to four subjects could be observed being put through rigorous exercise, their small bodies agile and strong despite their age.

"It seems rather premature to call him useless. He's still young." The subject in question wasn't even five years old and the only one to survive in the many batches of births for that year.

"The viable subjects have always manifested by this age. According to the numbers, more than ninety-five percent."

"From a still rather limited pool of candidates." A weak reply because Johan had also seen the stats. Those who didn't manifest until after they turned two almost invariably had health issues and died before the age of six. This project had been slowly moving along before he arrived on the scene.

"The ratio of no-shows has been getting worse since you took over," Mr. X pointed out.

"Because we've branched out. It's to be expected that modifications might take several tweaks to take proper effect."

"I've been more than patient. But obviously, *you* did something wrong. My understanding is that he's just the oldest current failure. We have more coming."

Johan fidgeted and hoped that Mr. X didn't notice him starting to sweat. "If I just had more time... I'm sure it's simply a matter of figuring out his trigger." The thing that would make the subject valuable. That would save his life.

"More time means more money. He needs to be removed to make room for other prospects."

And by *removed,* Mr. X didn't mean sending him to live elsewhere. A furnace was kept hot at all times to handle items that might cause trouble should the wrong people come across them.

Still, Johan Philips hadn't become the first doctor in his family so he could condone murder. "He's only a child."

"That's where you're wrong. He's a failure. *Your* failure. It would be a shame if you were to share his fate."

Johan swallowed hard. He knew that Mr. X wasn't being facetious. Everyone was well aware that the scientist who'd worked the project before him had died in a horrible car crash.

Despite what the reports claimed, it wasn't an accident.

Whose life mattered more? His or that of the subject created in a lab? The doctor pressed his lips tightly together and nodded. "It shall be as you command. I'll have him removed before the end of the day."

Mr. X turned from the window. "From now on, if

they don't manifest by the age of three, terminate them."

"That would eject two more children shortly," he exclaimed.

"I know. See it done." With that ominous order, Mr. X departed.

Yet Johan remained a while longer, staring at the little boy playing in the room. Healthy and bright. His only fault being too human.

Johan didn't visit the child until later that day. Heart heavy. Especially since subject DK04 smiled at the sight of him. "Hey, Dr. P."

Emotional, and his guilt almost enough to make him want to run, he did what he had to. The next time Mr. X. called and asked, "Did you get rid of the failure?" the doctor didn't have to lie when he said, "Yes."

Over the years, other children were removed, as well. None ever made it to the incinerator.

When Johan died in a car crash twenty-seven years later, he took that secret with him.

1

"Eat that cookie and die." The threat paused Dominick's hovering hand.

How had Mom heard him reaching for the cooling treat? To this day, Dominick envied her stealth skills. Even tried to emulate her and thought he'd done a fine job of sneaking.

Ninja-eared Mom heard him and now threatened with a metal spatula. From previous encounters with that lifter, he knew she would slap his hand if it moved.

Question being, was it worth the sting and her ire?

"Can't I have just one?" Yes, he whined. Anyone with taste buds would have begged for a cookie made by Nanette "Nana" Hubbard. His adoptive mother, giver of hugs, baker of cookies, currently in her avenging-kitchen-goddess mode.

Metal spatula in one hand, fingers curled around her cane with the other, at under five feet, Mom might be tiny, but she would still whoop his ass. No one made the mistake of thinking the tight gray curls and laugh lines made her weak. Nana Hubbard was a force of nature, and Dominick knew better than to ignore a warning.

But a cookie.

Hot from the oven.

Chocolate raisin oatmeal.

His favorite.

He needed one.

Needed. He almost growled the word. He'd had issues with his emotions lately. Too much pent-up energy inside.

And hunger. Add in a lack of impulse control, and he went for it!

The cookie he popped into his mouth burned and hurt almost as much as the whack. He'd endured worse abuse in his life, but never from his mom. She might give them the occasional slap when repeated warnings were ignored, but she never truly hurt Dominick or the other children. Nana barked more than she bit.

The worst trouble he'd ever gotten into happened in grade nine when he put that Smithers kid in the hospital. Call his sister a rude name? Like hell. Dominick never did tell his mom why he hurt the kid—Pammy didn't deserve having it repeated—and he bore the yanking of his ear and the yelling as she sent him to his room.

It was worth it. His sister hugged him and cried as she said, "Thank you." No thanks required. Adopted or not, Pammy was his sister, and he protected his family.

Later that night, Mom brought him up his favorite dessert and said, "Next time, don't get caught."

He didn't. But that violence, that outlet for his inner frustrations, pulsed more fiercely than before. It wanted an outlet. He found it in the military.

From the age of eighteen until two weeks ago, Dominick had served his country. Needed the structure. Learned to control the throbbing inside. As if something tried to crawl out.

For years, he'd thought he had it under control, and then once he hit his thirties, he found himself constantly battling inexplicable rage. Picking fights. Constantly in the gym when not in the field. But the black eyes and loose teeth weren't why people noticed that he had a problem.

Blame some shitty pot laced with something.

Dominick woke up about ten kilometers from camp, naked and covered in animal blood. Especially around his mouth. Just his luck, the military police for the camp found him, and they didn't sweep it under the rug.

It wasn't long before he found himself medically discharged. The doctors claimed PTSD, and that was it. Military career over.

Crushed, Dominick returned home because he had nowhere else to go. Given his constant deployments, he'd not bothered renting an apartment in a while.

Even now, home almost two weeks, and his shit remained boxed in the basement where it'd sat for years. Dominick only had the bare minimum in his old room, once shared with his brothers Stefan and Raymond. Now, it was just Dominick in the top bunk, which groaned ominously every time he climbed in. He really should dismantle it and turn the frame into something that could fit two singles side by side. He didn't, though, mostly because that would imply his situation was permanent.

Not really a bad thing, as it remained way more comfortable than some of the places he'd stayed. Under the faint glowing constellations on the ceiling, he slept more soundly than he had in years. If he ignored the strange dreams of running through forests and the hunting that didn't involve a gun.

But in good news, no blackouts. He remained drug and alcohol-free. Wouldn't even have a cigarette no matter how many times Stefan offered. Nicotine was a drug. He needed to remain in control.

Being home helped with that. There was tranquility in the familiar surroundings. It eased him to be around his family. Especially his mom, who loved to cook.

A good thing, too, because he found himself with a huge appetite. Since his return, Dominick was hungry all the time. Which was why, staring at the fresh cookies, the pain in his mouth and hand faded. He forgot all about the repercussions if he stole another.

Forget resisting. Those round, blissful bites would now be the perfect temperature.

Want.

He reached again and endured another smack.

One bite was all it took to find heaven. He groaned as his mom admonished, "Brat! Those are for the bake sale at Tyson's school." Tyson being his much younger brother. Sixteen going on attitude.

Dominick pulled a bill from his pocket and handed it over. "Will that buy me a third one?"

"You can have one more. And not the biggest," she added with a shake of her head.

Dominick snared a midsized cookie with lots of chocolate chips and took his time enjoying it, taking smaller bites as he watched Mom bustle around the kitchen.

Despite the cane she kept handy, she moved quite well, the stiffness in her right leg not slowing her down at all. But he worried.

They all did. He and his other siblings. More than most people had. At last count, nine, including him, with the youngest aged nine.

What would they have done if Mom had died in that car accident a few months ago?

"Stop staring at me." She caught him and chided.

"You sure you're okay?"

"Would you stop worrying? I'm fine. I'm just old. It takes longer to heal."

"If I ever get my hands on the person who ran that stop sign…" He growled. Deeply. Startlingly.

His mom eyed him. "You'll do nothing. Because the cops will do their jobs, and the culprit will be arrested and jailed. Don't you dare do anything that screws up our Thanksgiving dinner."

At the mention, he played aloof. "Depends. What are you making?"

"As if you care about anything but my tourtière," Mom scoffed.

She was right. He loved tourtière, the Quebecois version, with chunks of meat, potato, onions, and diced carrots. Cooked into a flaky crust that burst in the mouth along with the flavor of the spices and the gravy. The chunks of meat melted in the mouth. Mmm.

"You're dreaming of food again," Mom cajoled as she flipped cookies into a container.

"Fuck yeah, I am." Too many years of field rations had whetted his appetite.

"Language!"

That brought a tilt to his lips. "Please, I've heard you use worse."

"What happened to do as I say and not speak as I do?" Mom arched a brow.

"I think I'm old enough now to use whatever language I like."

"Oh, really?" his mother drawled. "We have young, impressionable ears in the house."

He snorted. "Have you heard Tyson when he's gaming online with his buddies?"

"Are you tattling on your brother?" More like an uncle given the age gap between them.

"The boy needs a firm guiding hand. Are you slipping, old lady?" He ducked before she could throw something at him and grinned at her snort.

"Don't you start. You know Tyson had a rough year. Last thing he needs is me harping on him all the time. Or are you telling me you're a better parent, Mr. Doesn't-even-own-a-dog?"

He wrinkled his nose. "Never will, either. And I guess you're a mostly awesome mom," he teased. His family was the only thing that could draw out the gentler side of him.

"Only mostly awesome?" she queried.

"Another cookie might change my mind." He tried and got shot down.

"Ha. See if I bake you the good stuff." She poked him in the belly. "From now on, only healthy options for you."

"So long as they have chocolate in them."

"Even the chicken I'm making for dinner?"

"Chicken?" His eyes lit. "What kind?" Because Mom made a mean deep-fried version with buttermilk batter that crunched with each bite. But she also had this version with a lemon sauce, ooh...and the one with the stuffing—

"Stop drooling. I haven't even put them in the oven yet." A massive, industrial-sized appliance that rarely *didn't* have something cooking. With nine kids, she'd learned to have massive amounts of food ready to eat at all times. Not a single leftover ever went to waste. Sunday was kitchen-sink day. All leftovers in the fridge had to go, and if there were none left? They had a pizza place on speed dial because Sunday was Mom's day of rest.

"How many are you expecting for dinner tonight?" It could vary wildly because, on any given night, his siblings might bring boyfriends and girlfriends. Mom always rose to the challenge, and no one ever left her table hungry. It helped that they lived on a farm with a few animals and some crops. Still, it didn't provide for everything.

"No idea. It's not like any of you give me any warning." She wrinkled her nose, but the grumble was half-hearted.

"You need a hand with anything?" he asked.

"Glad you asked." His mom gave him a smile that suddenly made him scared. So very scared. "I need a few things from the store."

Having played this game before, he knew a few things most likely meant a dozen, with specific brands. He held out his hand. "Give me the list."

"And waste paper?" She snorted. "I thought you were about saving the planet?"

"From bad guys."

"Well, now you can save it from waste and pollution." Mom whipped out her phone and began typing.

His cell dinged. "I assume that's the list."

"Yup. You can take my van."

"Lucky me." Because nothing said *big, bad, retired military guy* like driving a sky-blue minivan with a bumper sticker that said: *If you can read this, I hope you have a nice day.*

Emasculating.

"You're welcome. The shopping bins are stacked in the back."

"Bins? How many groceries we talking about?"

He pulled out his phone and tapped, opening the text she'd sent with a link. His eyes widened. "What the ever-loving fuck is this?"

"The grocery list. And because I'm nice, I've placed the items in a spreadsheet separated by store, included the aisle, price, and quantity." The organization took her craziness to a new level.

"Are you sure this is right? It's massive." As in might as well just toss a store on top of the van and drive it home big.

"Are you not up to the challenge? Perhaps your little brother is better suited for the task."

Despite recognizing the insult, he still bristled. Dominick straightened. "I can handle this. It's just groceries."

"A few days before Thanksgiving. And you, a rookie." She shook her head. "Maybe I should go myself."

He tucked the phone away. "How hard can it be?"

Harder than expected when the cranberry shelf only had two dented cans left, and three people vying for them.

Surely, the can of cherries would suffice. He also didn't get pumpkin pie filling, and this despite being in his third grocery store.

According to someone who heard him muttering about it, shelves had been harder to keep stocked since the COVID-19 pandemic. Businesses went under. Shipping had slowed.

It might be why he'd gone a little overboard buying boxes of treats at his last stop. In his defense, it was hard to decide. Chocolate cake with vanilla frosting or vanilla cake? What about the one with coconut or the honey-glazed donuts? He bought two of each. By having his own sweets stash, he could avoid getting his hand slapped.

The line to the checkout was a snaking affair with spots marked for social distancing. Most people followed them, but a few crowded. When someone touched the backs of his heels with their cart, he turned and bared his teeth. His ankles didn't get an apology, but the buggy didn't hit him again.

As Dominick neared the checkout with his overflowing cart, he saw a woman behind the Plexiglas shield for the cashier. Her dirty-blonde hair was pulled back in a ponytail, her nose and cheeks as freckled as ever.

His heart literally skipped a beat.

"Holy shit, is that you, Anika?"

Her hazel gaze met his, and it took a second and a frown before she muttered, "Dominick?"

"Yeah, from high school. Remember me?"

Her lips quirked. "I do." Her gaze dropped from his face to his gut, reminding him of the time she'd slugged him. He'd gotten drunk at a party and suggested they have sex. Actually, what he'd said was, *"Hey, honey, you look good enough to lick."*

She'd declined. So, he'd doubled down and said, *"Well, if I can't taste you, then feel free to suck me."*

She'd gut-punched him and said, *"You're disgusting."*

Well-deserved. And he'd been contrite when he sobered up. Even tried to make amends. She'd flipped him the bird.

That'd led to him having the biggest crush on her the rest of his time in school. A crush unrequited.

To this day, she didn't appear impressed. She ignored him as she ran his items over the scanner.

"So, what have you been up to?" he asked.

"Working."

"Me too. Military."

"Good for you." Mumbled without looking up.

A glance at her hand showed no ring, but that didn't mean shit. "How you been?"

Rather than answer, she kept scanning. Within Dominick, a familiar frustration bubbled. What the fuck was her problem?

"You always this happy, or did I catch you on your period?" Regret hit the moment the words left his mouth.

She cast him a glare. "You always a big jerk, or is this my lucky day?"

"I wouldn't be a jerk if you weren't being a bitch."

Uh-oh.

Her gaze narrowed. "Wow, with a shining personality like yours, it must cost you a fortune to convince hookers to date you."

His jaw dropped, and in that moment, something odd happened.

The rage within flipped to lust. Which led to him saying, "A thousand bucks for the night. I'll even pay for the room."

2

Did he just—?

No.

He didn't.

Fucker, he did.

"I am not a whore," she snapped.

"Never said you were."

"You just offered me money to have sex," she hissed.

"I take it that's a no?"

If it hadn't been for the Plexiglas shield, she would have slapped him.

"You're disgusting."

"You were the one saying I had to buy it."

"Because I have a hard time believing you could be charming enough to convince anyone to go on a date with you." Not entirely the truth. He was handsome enough that many women would likely ignore his misogynistic mouth. Not her, though.

"I don't need to be charming, I'm big." He puffed out his chest.

She blinked at his arrogance. "Then go on a diet."

He stared at her. "I am not fat."

"You're the one who said you were big." She should have stuck to being quiet, but nope, she just had to rise to his goading.

"I meant it as in big where it counts. You know. Down there."

"I know what you meant, and I still can't believe you said it. Like, seriously? What part of *not interested* do you not understand?" Men could be absolute pigs, and she'd know. They seemed to think that just because she worked behind the conveyor belt, they could say anything they wanted to her.

He blustered. "What is your problem with me?"

"I haven't seen you in nearly two decades, and you think offering me money to whore myself and telling me you have a big dick the first time we talk is appropriate?" She arched a brow. "Guess again." She kept scanning his snack food. Box after box.

Despite her calling him overweight, she could tell —even with his loose, plaid shirt—he was actually in pretty good shape. Must be nice to be able to eat whatever you liked. Anika struggled with her weight, and even though she kept to a strict diet and exercise regimen, she'd never be petite.

But some people didn't grasp that. She'd been subjected to: "Do you really need that second helping? Perhaps you should skip dessert" her entire life.

Maybe people should mind their own fucking business. She was big-boned, which meant wider and thicker than some girls. But she wasn't fat. She exercised every day. Her stomach was flat, her arms and legs strong.

"Sorry if I offended you." Stiffly said. Not sincere at all.

She snorted. "As if I care. Do you know how many guys think it's okay to say stuff like that to me? And don't get me started on the women."

"If you don't like the job, then change it."

Her spine straightened. "Excuse me, don't you dare put me and what pays my bills down."

His mouth rounded. "You were just saying people were mean to you."

She angry-bagged his items. "To make a point that I'm used to jerks like you coming in here and thinking you can talk to me any way you like. And it's not okay. Do you hear me? Not. Okay."

"Um, Anika, can I have a word?" She whirled to see Darryl, the store manager, standing at the end of her register.

"Oh, shit," she muttered.

"It's okay, we know each other," Dominick stated to her manager.

"Actually, it's not," Darryl said firmly. He was only a few years out of high school and trying hard not to look intimidated by the big guy he confronted.

"And I say it is. I said something rude to her, and she rightly called me on it." Dominick loomed over the guy. "So, don't you dare fire her."

Darryl almost smirked before catching himself. "I'm not firing her, sir. I was removing her from an unsafe situation. Mainly, you."

Dominick's gaze widened. "I'm not threatening her."

"You're being disrespectful to an employee, and we don't allow that. Please leave."

"I will once I pay for my groceries," Dominick stated.

"Now." Darryl might have tiny balls, but they were full of courage.

"I can't leave now. My mom needs this shit." Dominick pulled out his credit card. "I swear I'll behave."

"It's okay, Darryl. Let the guy buy his snack cakes," Anika jumped in.

When her manager would have likely insisted, Anika kept scanning items and finishing Dominick's order. "That's two hundred and twenty-two dollars and eighty-four cents."

He blinked. "For cake?"

"What did you expect?"

"I don't know. Until recently, I was eating in mess halls or restaurants. At home, food usually just appears on a plate."

She rolled her eyes. "Spoiled."

"I don't know if I'd say that. I spent six months in the desert sucking the moisture from plants and eating what rodents and insects I could catch."

"Why?" she couldn't help but blurt out.

"My mission got sidetracked. It took a while for extraction."

"I meant why serve in the military if it's that awful?" she asked as the receipt spit out, his credit card having worked.

"Because I was good at it."

"Was? Did you retire?"

"I did."

"So, you're here for a visit?" She couldn't have said why she asked—as if she cared what his jerk ass did.

"Not sure yet what my plan is. Still adjusting to civilian life."

Rather than snort and tell him that he needed to work a heck of a lot more and harder on it, she said, "Good luck with that. Have a good day." She turned from him and began greeting her next customer, but he wouldn't budge.

"Hey, I don't suppose you'd like to go to dinner or grab a coffee sometime?"

She laughed so hard she snorted.

"Is that a no?" he asked.

"It's a never." Because the last thing she needed was to date some guy who thought women should serve. She'd done that once before and ended up in divorce court with everything, including the dog, taken from her. So unfair given Thomas stopped working a few months into their marriage. Everything they'd had was because of her, but the law gave him half. Plus, she got stuck paying the lawyer fees, leaving her with nothing. Not even the ability to work in her field because the prick filed a false complaint and she lost her dental hygienist's license.

Now, she worked at a grocery store, lived in a shitty apartment with secondhand crap, hadn't dated in two years, and her vibrator had broken from too much use and she couldn't afford to replace it.

Perhaps she shouldn't have been so rash with Dominick.

Didn't some fetish exist where the guy had his mouth taped shut? If he didn't speak, she could just use him for sex.

Ha.

The very idea.

She might be many things but a girl who slept around for the sake of lust wasn't one of them. She might have been burned once, but she still believed in love.

And she'd promised herself to always demand respect.

3

THAT DIDN'T GO WELL.

As he loaded the grocery bins into the van, Dominick pondered the many ways the conversation with Anika had gone wrong.

So wrong. No wonder she'd shot him down.

In his defense, she addled his wits.

Meeting Anika proved to be a punch to the gut. For one, she remained as attractive as ever with her curvy frame. While some liked their women thin, Dominick had always been more attracted to bigger girls. The kind that could handle a large guy like him. Something to grab on to.

The second thing that hit him hard was just how strongly the lust hit at the sight of her. Blame the blood leaving his brain, headed for his dick that led to the supremely stupid shit he'd said to her.

But she bore some of the blame. From the beginning, even though he'd been nice, she'd acted snootily. Like she was better than him.

Her loss. Plenty of other women out there that wouldn't mind a retired military guy with a decent pension. Once he got a job, he'd have even more to offer.

Arriving home, Dominick began pulling out his stash. As he brought it in, he ran into his little brother Tyson, whose eyes widened.

"What did you do?" the boy breathed. He'd chosen to shave his wiry hair short on the sides but had left it thick and teased on top.

"Got groceries like Mom asked."

Tyson pointed at the boxes peeking from a grocery bin. "That's junk food."

"I know. I bought it."

"But Nana says we can't have it." Tyson shook his head. The boy had decided once he hit his teens that he was too mature to call her *Mom*.

"It's no different than the cakes and cookies she makes. This will save her some work." And keep him from getting slapped when the hunger hit.

Tyson backed away. "She's gonna kill you."

Actually, she did worse than that. Mom saw the goods as he put them in the pantry.

Her lips wobbled, and she wailed, "Is my baking that bad?"

Dominick shook a box at her. "You know I love your shit. But you are supposed to be taking it easy." He pointed to her leg. "Sit. Relax. I got the dessert part covered."

His mom shuddered. "That is not dessert. It's processed poison. Is this what you've been eating while you've been away from home?"

"Maybe," he hedged.

"I blame myself. I must have gone wrong somewhere with you." She could be dramatic when needed.

"You raised me just fine."

"Did I? Because you're the oldest and still unmarried." She eyed him.

"I haven't had time to date much."

"That was before. You're out of the military now. So, what is your plan?"

He blinked. "I need a plan?"

"You're not getting any younger, Dom." She patted his cheek.

"I'm only thirty-seven."

"Only? If you want to be able to keep up with toddlers, you'd better get working on an heir."

"Why are you bugging me? I just got home. Bug Stefan or Raymond. What about Pammy?" He couldn't explain to his mom that he worried his rage would worsen. Look at his reaction with Anika today. He'd rather die than hurt a kid.

"Don't deflect. It's time you settled down. Which is why I've invited someone to dinner. She's very nice. A few years younger than you. Healthy."

"She sounds like a broodmare."

"Nothing wrong with choosing a healthy partner to bear your babies."

Dominick groaned. "Must you say the word babies?"

"Yes, because someone needs to give me some!" She flung out her arms and stalked away. He couldn't help but follow, peeling the wrapper from a treat.

She whirled and visibly shuddered at the sight of him. "Garbage. Ugh."

Worst part? He agreed. Her cakes and icings were much tastier.

"Who is this woman that will wow me with her genetics?" he asked, leaning against the counter as Mom opened the oven to baste the row of chickens.

"You'll see."

He did. A lovely lady, thirty-one, never married but who had been in a serious relationship for years. She had excellent manners. A tiny laugh. Pretty hair. And a slim figure.

Too slim.

He couldn't help but think of Anika.

"Are you thinking of food again?" his mother asked as what's her name went to the bathroom.

"Not exactly." However, he would eat Anika in a heartbeat if she gave him permission.

After a perfectly fine dessert, where what's-her-name dazzled with her boringness, he finally saw her to the door and sighed as it shut.

His mom glared at him. "What was wrong with Veronica?"

"Absolutely nothing."

"Then why don't you like her?"

"She's not the one."

"Don't tell me you suddenly believe in love?" Mom snorted.

"Would you really want me to make a baby with a stranger, or someone I connect with?"

She pursed her lips. "You had thirty-seven years to connect. Now it's my turn."

He sighed. "It's not that easy."

"Says you."

She didn't understand the turmoil within him. Could he really saddle anyone with that?

"I need to go for a walk and work off that excellent dinner." He patted his stomach. Hard. Not fat. Still, he couldn't forget what Anika had implied. "Do I look chubby to you?"

The snort Mom uttered acted as a reply. He went for a jog nonetheless and travelled far enough that he passed by the grocery store, still open with a single cashier inside.

Anika.

Working late.

He'd planned to do a few more kilometers before returning home. Instead, he turned around and came back, bouncing on the balls of his feet in place as he drew up level with the grocery store. He was just in time to see Anika walking to a lone car at the far end of the parking lot.

She had her head ducked and hands shoved into her pockets, seemingly unaware of the space around her, thus never seeing the gang of boys that approached.

Or did she? He noticed her stiffen, and she whirled before they got close enough to grab her.

"I have nothing," she declared preemptively. "Unless you want a piece-of-shit car that only runs half the time."

The thugs spread out, and the guy with the leather jacket cajoled. "Keep your bucket of rust. I'm more interested in your mouth, slut."

The second of his buddies guffawed, while the third grabbed at his crotch and thrust his hips.

Rude motherfuckers.

Dominick had seen enough. He began walking toward the group, even as Anika faced off with them.

"Hey, assholes, did your father not teach you to respect a lady?" Dominick spoke loudly enough for them to hear.

Two of them whirled. The one with a tattoo above his brow sneered. "Mind your fuckin' business."

"She is my business." He stopped and hooked his thumbs through the belt loops in his pants.

"I don't need your help," Anika muttered.

"You heard the bitch. She don't need—argh!"

On hearing the word *bitch*, Dominick moved and had the tattooed fellow in a headlock as he growled, "Do not call her a bitch. She is a lady, you fucking punk."

It took Tattoo's friends a second to snap out of their shock and attack. With one arm around Tattoo's neck, Dom used his other hand to catch a flying fist. He squeezed it, and the guy screamed as something cracked. The third fellow kicked him.

In the shin.

"Ow?" Dominick mocked with an arched brow. He tossed Tattoo at the kicker, and they both went stumbling and fell to the ground.

Dominick turned around to the crunched-fist fellow and said, "You done?"

Apparently, all three of them were because they picked themselves off the pavement and took off running.

Turning to Anika, Dominick expected gratitude. Some admiration maybe. Perhaps a softening toward him—finally.

But no.

She glared with lips pressed tight. "What the hell was that macho bullshit about?"

"You're welcome."

"I had the situation under control."

That brought a disparaging noise to his lips. "How do you figure that? Can you not count? Because I did. It was three against you."

"I can protect myself."

"Can you?" For some reason, her stubborn refusal to be gracious annoyed him. He invaded her space, and while most women shied away when he loomed, Anika tilted her chin to look him in the eye.

"I don't need you playing savior."

"Would it kill you to say thank you?"

"Thank you."

It sounded about as sincere as his apology that afternoon. For some reason, he sighed. "Why is it that, when I'm around you, I never say the right thing?"

"Because you're an ass?" she offered.

"Not usually."

"Meaning there must be something wrong with me." She snorted. "Your ego is so huge I'm surprised you can carry it around."

"Why do you hate me so much?"

"I don't hate you."

He laughed, the sound holding a hint of ruefulness. "Yeah, you do."

"Guess you're not my cup of tea." One of the most annoying expressions of this decade, and she used it on him.

It could mean only one thing. His lips rounded as he exhaled. "You're a lesbian."

He never saw the fist that knocked him flat.

4

"FUCK ME! YOU BROKE MY NOSE." HE MOANED.

Anika didn't feel bad about it at all, even as she couldn't believe she'd landed it.

She didn't apologize.

As Dominick lay on the ground blinking, his nose bleeding, she stood over him and snapped, "I don't like you because you're an arrogant ass. And for your information, I like men. Nice men. Not jerks who think they're God's gift to women."

With that, she stepped over him and got into her car. She began driving away, only to pass him, walking diagonally across the lot with his hand still held over his nose. She turned onto the road and kept seeing him, moving on foot, bleeding.

Fuck.

Fuck a duck.

Fuck!

She turned around and pulled up beside him before rolling down the window. "You going to be okay?"

"Eventually."

Not usually a violent person, and very Canadian, she couldn't help but say, "I'm sorry I broke your nose."

"No, you're not." To her surprise, the statement emerged thickly but not angrily. Dominick's wry expression met hers as he ducked to peer inside the car.

"Okay, I'm not sorry. You asked for it. Seriously, who the fuck calls someone a lesbian just because she's not interested?"

"An asshole. I'm sorry. Guess I lost my manners while in the bush." He still had a liquid rattle to his words.

"Where's your car? Can you drive?"

"No car. I was jogging."

"I'll drive you to the hospital."

He snorted and winced. "No hospital. But I would take a ride home."

"Where do you live?"

As he named the road, her brows lifted. He lived more than ten kilometers from the store. "That seems like a long jog," she stated as she sped up to make a light.

"Not really. I usually run farther."

"Every day?"

"Whenever I can since I came home. Mom says I've got too much energy from boredom."

"Must be nice to have the time," she muttered.

He heard. "I'm not used to it. In the military, when I wasn't prepping for an exercise, I was on a mission or being debriefed. My days had structure."

"And you liked that?" She wrinkled her nose. She'd hate to have someone telling her what to do.

"It's easy to follow orders."

"I'm sure wherever you end up working, you'll have plenty to keep you happy." She couldn't have said why she was being nice. He didn't deserve it.

He was a veteran.

Dammit. She didn't want to cut him any slack, but she did have to recognize that he'd been living a vastly different life than she had for a while now. A rougher existence. But that didn't mean she'd give him a free pass.

"Guess now that my career is over, I need to figure out my next job." Said flatly.

"Do you want one?" she asked. "I mean, I kind of assumed." Perhaps he couldn't work. She didn't know if he'd left the service for medical reasons.

She'd hate to think that he was just lazy and wanted to live off the government's tit.

"Of course, I want to work!" he burst out. "But I have no skills outside the military. I feel so fucking useless. And now I sound like a pussy for admitting it. Jesus. Why can't I stop running my mouth around you?" He looked out the side window as she turned onto the road for his house.

"Have you talked to someone about how you've been feeling since you retired?"

"I do not want a head shrink," he growled, the vowels low and rumbly.

"Well, excuse me," she said with exaggerated annoyance. "Didn't realize it was so fucking shameful." She'd seen one for a while after the divorce until she discovered CBD oil. Bye-bye stress.

"It's just...a shrink can't fix what's wrong with me because it's not only in my head."

"Are you injured?" she asked.

"Not exactly. There's something wrong inside, and they can't find it."

"Don't give up," she advised as she turned into a driveway that led to a farm of all places. The massive gravel lane was a few hundred yards long and opened into a massive space in front of a white plank farmhouse, the kind that had been built onto over the years and had odd angles to it, along with a wraparound porch.

As she pulled up, Dominick muttered, "Thanks."

"I hope you get your shit together," she offered.

"Me, too." He offered her a wry grin, the first she'd seen from him, and the transformation hit her in the gut.

"Do you need any help getting inside?" she asked as he pulled on the handle to open the door.

He laughed. "No. I'm emasculated enough imagining the mockery my brothers will throw my way when they find out you decked me."

"You're not going to lie and say it was that gang?"

"Family doesn't lie to one another. And they also never let you live shit down." With a long-suffering sigh, Dominick got out of the car. Someone leaning against a post pushed away and drawled, "What the fuck happened to you?"

"She did." Dominick pointed right at her.

"You got decked by a girl?" The laughter proved boisterous enough that it drew an older woman outside. She clutched a cane as she emerged onto the porch.

"Dommy! What happened to your face?"

"It's okay, Mom. Just being taught some manners."

"By who?" his mom huffed.

Time to leave. Only he'd yet to close the passenger-side door. Anika leaned over to grab the armrest but lacked the arm length to reach.

"Hey. Mind closing the door?" Anika whisper-shouted to him.

Before he could move, his mom yelled, "Have you said thank you for the ride home?"

Dominick's gaze met hers, flaring for a second before his eyelids partially lowered. "Thanks for the ride."

"Invite them in."

"I don't think Anika wants to stay."

"You haven't even asked."

The argument made her think of a horror movie.

I'm that stupid girl.

Only in that second did it occur to her that she might have made a mistake coming to his place. She'd thought only of doing the right thing. Yet she'd taken a rude and angry ex-soldier alone in her car to a remote location.

She should have texted someone. Taken a picture of him. Something. What if his family were cannibals?

"Mom, she doesn't want to stay. Who do you think hit me?"

Dominick slammed the door shut, and she let out a breath as she sat up and put her foot on the brake. She shifted and went to hit the gas, only to notice a young woman standing in front of the car, her purple hair cut in a short shag. She glared at Anika, arms crossed over her chest. Obviously, not letting her leave.

Finally, recovering her wits, Anika pulled out her phone and did a direct picture posted to social media, tagging her location. If she disappeared, they'd know where to start looking.

Then Anika got out of the car. "Is there a reason you're not letting me leave?"

"You hit my brother."

"He deserved it." The truth.

The girl snapped. "He's a veteran. Who's been through enough."

"He was an ass who should have walked home. But I was being nice."

"Leave her alone." All eyes flicked to Dominick, who shifted uncomfortably. "Um. Er. It was just a misunderstanding."

As he hemmed and hawed, Anika couldn't stand it.

She jabbed a finger in his direction. "Don't you dare try and minimize what you did. He called me a lesbian because I wouldn't drop my panties for him. So, I hit him."

If she'd expected his family to be pissed, she was wrong. The bearded guy on the porch laughed, while the purple-haired girl nodded. "Good for you. I'd have flattened him, too."

Whereas the old lady eyed her up and down and said, "Do you like cookies?"

Before Anika could reply, the purple-haired girl did. "You'll regret it if you say no. Nana Hubbard is the best cook you'll ever meet."

"I can't. I should get home."

"Husband? Children? Pet?" Mrs. Hubbard fired questions at her.

"None of the above. It's been a long day. I worked a twelve-hour shift."

Mrs. Hubbard's expression brightened. "A hardworking girl like you needs food. Come. I have something."

Dominick appeared surprised, which didn't alleviate her discomfort. "I shouldn't."

It was the purple-haired girl who said it aloud. "I swear, we're not planning to dismember and freeze you for food or turn you into a broodmare to form a hillbilly army."

Way to read her mind. "Isn't that exactly what a murdering hillbilly daughter would say?" She'd yet to close her car door. She could still jump in and run people over.

"Jesus fucking Christ. She wants to go. Let her go. I can't believe you want to feed her. I'm the injured party here," Dominick pouted.

"You disrespected her," Mrs. Hubbard chided, and he hung his head.

"I'm sorry."

"Don't apologize to me. She's the one who needs it." His mom pointed at Anika.

Anika lifted her hands. "It's fine. Whatever. I'm sure he's learned his lesson."

"I can't believe a son of mine would act in such a manner," Mrs. Hubbard declared, and he shrank even further.

Anika almost felt sorry for him. "The military changes people, I hear."

His mom snorted. "You're being too polite. Which is why I won't take no for an answer. You're coming in for a snack."

The woman insisted, and Anika knew she shouldn't, yet her feet, driven by curiosity, moved.

"Let her go home. She doesn't want to be here," Dominick protested.

"The girl needs food, and I need someone to do the dishes."

"You have a dishwasher," he pointed out.

"Not good enough. I want hand-washed dishes. Hand-dried, too," Nana declared as she marched into the house.

"Ignore them. I'm Maeve." Anika found herself led to the porch steps by the purple-haired girl, who linked her arm with Anika's.

Anika hesitated near the first step.

"It's okay. You won't die. Promise." Maeve

propelled her forward. "Welcome to the insanity. As I said, I'm Maeve, Dom's sister. You met Mom—Nana—and the guy sucking back cancer is my other brother, Stefan. And you are?"

Seriously confused.

5

Holy fucking mess. And Dominick wasn't talking about his nose.

His emotions seesawed. Pissed. Incredulous. Hurt. Horny. And all of them because of Anika, who was now in his house, which meant cookies or cake. Maybe even Mom's special hot cocoa.

The thoughts of a yummy snack drowned out the warning bells until too late. By the time the door slammed shut, and Anika was sitting on a kitchen stool, he'd missed his window to send her on her way.

Panic stilled his heart as his mom, a determined look in place, set to work on Anika.

"What's your name?" Mom asked as she slid a plate in front of Anika, the surface covered with thin slices of roast beef, a chunk of ham, cherry tomatoes, and cheese.

"Anika."

Looked yummy. When he would have joined them, his mother shot him a look. "Clean yourself up first. This is not a boxing ring."

He did the fastest face wash and shirt change ever and, in less than a minute, pounded back down the stairs, only to run into his brother Stefan at the bottom.

Stefan hung onto the newel as he drawled, "When do you want lessons on what *not* to say to a woman?"

"Fuck off."

"Don't get pissy with me. I'm not the one calling women lesbians because they don't like my caveman tactics."

"Again, fuck off." Dominick didn't need his suave brother rubbing his face in his failure. He'd not spent most of his adult life chasing skirts like Stefan had. He'd been serving his country. He didn't have time to flirt and charm. Sex was mostly about filling a need, and those kinds of women didn't expect or need sweet talk.

"You get better results if you fuck on," was the teasing reply, "but that will only happen if you learn to control your temper, brother. You are like a powder keg, always ready to go off."

He felt it, too. Even now, the rage bubbled, as did a pacing anxiousness to get back to Anika. What had his mom said to her by now? What was she eating? Would she share?

"I don't need your advice."

"If you say so, bro. But if you change your mind, you know my address."

His Casanova brother had a condo in downtown Ottawa, but he visited the farmhouse regularly.

Dominick paced past him, heading for the kitchen in time to see Anika's face as she took her first bite of Mom's famous flaky pastry filled with a homemade cherry jam and fresh whipped cream.

Pure rapture filled Anika's expression. He stumbled to a halt and stared as she chewed with obvious enjoyment. Then licked her lips. Missed a crumb that looked delicious—

His mom hip-checked him as she moved past, still talking to Anika. "Tell me, Anika, where do you live?"

"Beckwith."

"But you work at…" His mom had a way of interrogating that got results.

"The Food Basics in Richmond." A recent build that hadn't existed the last time he'd spent a few weeks at home.

"You have family in the area?"

Anika shook her head. "My parents are alive, but

I don't see them often since they moved to Florida. When they're not down there, they tend to go stay with my sister in BC."

"What's wrong with visiting you here?" Dominick asked, breaking the repartee and drawing her gaze.

She rolled her shoulders. "Shittier weather, a pullout couch, one bathroom, and the fact I am a disappointment to them."

"Assholes," he said vehemently.

Anika's lips quirked. "Yes, they are. Which is why it's not a big loss."

"Fuck 'em."

Mom smacked Dominick. "Be nice. Or she has my permission to hit you again."

"Ouch. Fine. I'll behave." He cowered, mostly because he caught Anika trying to hide a smile.

It was the first one he'd managed to coax. He preferred it to her scowl.

His mom bustled off, and with her back to him while at the stove, he leaned close and whispered to Anika, "Can I have a bite?" He'd noticed not one, not two, but *three* dessert treats on her plate.

She eyed the pastry in her hand and then him before uttering a pert, "Nope." Then she ate the whole thing, her expression dancing with mirth as he groaned in disappointment.

His mom caught it as she turned around. "Don't

you be stealing her treats. You've been a naughty boy."

"You got told." Anika snickered.

Way to emasculate him further.

"Did you at least tell Mom how I saved you from a gang of thugs?" He tried to redeem himself.

"I would have handled it."

"There were three of them." He pointed out the math.

"Who turned out to be cowards. Usually, once you take out the ringleader, the others lose interest."

"Got a lot of experience taking down gangs?" he drawled.

"I work late a few days a week. Do you think this is the first time I've had a problem?" She arched a brow.

The very idea that she'd had to defend herself before didn't sit well.

"You should find a safer place to work then. Or demand day shifts."

She laughed. "Yeah, because I work nights at the grocery store because it's my dream. Some of us have to do whatever it takes to pay the bills. We don't get to dictate terms."

"You should have someone walk you to your car, then."

"I don't need a man to protect me," was her icy reply.

"You tell him, sister!" was Maeve's proclamation as she emerged from the pantry with her hands full.

"What are you doing?" he asked as his sister set a bunch of strange shit on the counter. Vegan vanilla-flavored protein powder. Walnuts. Some weird green powdery crap. All dumped into a blender, along with ice and almond milk to make vomit.

Seriously. Bilious green vomit was what she poured into a glass.

"Want some?" Maeve offered, to which Anika shook her head and Dominick uttered an, "Ew."

As for Mom, she made the sign of the cross despite not being religious.

They all watched with horrified fascination as Maeve held it to her lips and chugged. Then waited to see if it would come back up.

Maeve burped and grinned. "So healthy."

"So gross." Stefan wandered into the kitchen and snared a cookie without losing a hand.

Dominick could only stare hopefully, but he was still in trouble.

"You're all related?" Anika asked.

Dominick could understand her confusion, seeing as not one of them looked anything like the other.

"Yes."

"No."

At the opposing answers from Stefan and Maeve, Mom explained. "All my children are orphans."

"How many do you have?" Anika asked, eating a brownie next, her groan of rapture not unnoticed by him.

He felt himself getting lightheaded as his blood headed south.

"Nine. Dommy is the oldest."

"And still living at home," Anika muttered.

"Temporarily." He felt a need to bluster.

His mom failed to help with her addition of, "Only until my precious boy finds a good woman to settle down with and pops out some babies."

Anika choked—not because of the brownie he'd wager.

He glared at his mom. She smiled over Anika's bent and coughing form.

Dominick pressed his lips tight and shook his head.

Mother smiled. "Here. Have some hot cocoa, dear." She pressed a hot mug with floating marshmallows and a sprinkle of cinnamon on top into Anika's hands.

The foam on Anika's upper lip after a sip almost saw her ravished on the kitchen floor.

What the fuck was wrong with him?

He shoved out of his seat and headed for the fridge. Would anyone think it weird if he stuck his head into the freezer for a few minutes?

"Do you have any grandkids?" Anika asked as

Dominick pretended to look for something. He found the Popsicles he'd bought earlier.

"No grandbabies yet. Everyone's too busy with their careers," his mom huffed. "Although I'm hoping Dom will settle down now that he's not busy running off and playing war games."

"Playing?" He snorted, coming out of the freezer with a Popsicle in each hand. "Peace missions are not fun and games."

"But they do keep you away from home."

"Not anymore." He was still bitter about it. Forced to retire because they thought him medically unfit.

"So, what are you doing now that you're retired?" If anyone but Anika had asked, he might have snapped.

He shrugged. "I don't know."

"He needs to get a job," was his mother's advice.

"Know anyone looking for a soldier?" he asked, half joking.

"The only thing our store is looking for is a shelf stocker." Anika rolled her shoulders as she ate the last dessert, a chocolate rum ball rolled in coconut.

He grimaced, mostly because he hated that she licked her own lips. "Shelf stocking sounds boring." He almost said *demeaning* but caught himself at the last second before she could slap him again.

"Boring pays the bills," was Anika's pert reply as

she stood. "Thank you for the meal. It was nice meeting you."

As Anika moved for the front door, Mom's death glare hit him, and he didn't need words to know that he should see her out. Dominick followed her up the hall and stood awkwardly to the side as Anika slipped on her shoes.

"Thanks for the ride."

The corner of her mouth lifted. "Considering I got fed, it's *me* who should say thanks. Your mom can cook."

"She sure can." The dumbest thing to reply. And given his added discomfort, he stuffed his hands into his pockets.

"Bye, Dominick." She headed down the steps to her car, and he followed.

"I don't suppose you might have changed your mind about getting a coffee now that you've met my family."

She paused before getting into the vehicle. He expected her to say no. But, to his surprise, she said, "Okay."

Wait, she said *yes*? Before he could say anything—likely a good thing since it would have probably involved his foot in his mouth—she was gone. He stayed, staring after her long enough that his brother noticed.

Stefan, with his smart mouth, emerged to say, "Damn, she is a fine piece of ass."

Wham.

The pussy went whining to Mom. "Dommy broke my nose!"

And he'd break it again if Stefan ever talked about Anika like that in front of him.

6

THE MOMENT SHE AGREED TO COFFEE, Anika regretted it. Despite all the evidence to the contrary, Dominick probably took it to mean that she was interested.

To her disgust, she was. Kind of. But mostly, it was a means to get out of her rut. She'd barely dated since the divorce years ago. Guy-shy. Busy. Scared. Not interested.

Most men barely registered on her radar. But Dominick? He annoyed her. Even as he exuded some kind of vibe that made her want to climb him like a tree.

Maybe she should have said yes to the thousand bucks. She could have used the money. Especially since she never seemed to get ahead. Just like she barely lived. Work, clean, sleep. That was her life.

Boring.

So fucking boring.

When was the last time she'd done something fun? Bingeing a show on Netflix didn't count.

Why did everything have to suck so bad?

Entering her shitty apartment, she couldn't help but grit her teeth and ball her fists. It was unfair how Thomas had taken everything from her. How had a guy who'd always had an excuse for why he had to quit his job conned a judge into giving him everything he asked for? Including alimony.

Since she'd been fired as a dental hygienist, though—because Thomas had filed a false report of sexual misconduct—she'd had the alimony revoked. Because in an ironic twist, she no longer made enough to pay it.

Which pissed Thomas off. Enough that he'd been coming around lately to harass her. Apparently, the restraining order wasn't worth the paper it was written on.

Asshole. She sure seemed to attract them, even as she couldn't figure out what Dominick saw in her.

She lacked the petite or willowy figures most guys preferred. She didn't wear makeup often. Her hair was long and simple, usually pulled back from her face.

As she stared at her reflection, she couldn't help but think that she'd given up.

No. That wasn't true.

She just didn't give a shit anymore. Not about how she looked anyhow.

And despite that, Dominick kept flirting with her, if you could call his crude attempts flirting. His saving grace?

His family. He must have some redeeming features, given they still seemed to like him. His mom came across as nice. His sister, too. Anika had not known him well in high school. The first time they met after she'd moved into the area, he'd been crude at that party, and she'd hit him. Then, she'd avoided him out of embarrassment.

Almost twenty years later, he was still crude. But apologetic.

Why was she still thinking about him?

Fatigued, she should have been collapsing into bed. Instead, restless, she flung back the covers, dropped her panties, and pulled her knees up and to the sides.

Licking a finger to moisten it, she slid it between her legs.

A quick stroke over her clit, and she trembled.

Most definitely overdue.

Her slick finger worked her clit, slipping back and forth. Knowing the right kind of pressure. The right type of touch.

She had her eyes closed, but for the first time, she saw a face.

Dominick's.

Her breath hitched as she imagined him touching her.

Would he be a rough lover? Or the kind that seemed gruff and tough but was tender in bed?

Arousal moistened her sex, giving her all the lube she needed to keep playing. But tonight, fingers wouldn't be enough.

Rolling to her side, she found her broken vibrator in the drawer. It didn't shake or roll, but it had the length and width to fill.

She ran the head of it over her clit before slipping it into her sex.

She seesawed it back and forth, shoving it deep. Letting it fill her.

Pushing it against the spot that brought a hiccup of pleasure.

In and out she shoved, panting as she thrust. Imagining him above her. Covering her. Fucking her.

Tension coiled within until it burst. She came with a gasp, rippling with pleasure. Breathing hard.

Then, she lay there unsatisfied. Because it just wasn't the same as the real thing.

A sex toy couldn't hug.

7

Anika had said yes to coffee, and Dominick couldn't have said why it excited him. But his mom noticed.

"You're jumpier than a cat on a metal roof," she proclaimed the next morning as she whipped out various breakfasts and packed some lunches—the two younger kids had school.

"Would you believe I'm nervous?" He didn't mention the real reason and went with, "I haven't had to apply for a job in years." And rather than print out a resume and hand it out to businesses, Raymond had submitted applications for him online. Apparently, paper was a thing of the past.

Fucking technology.

"You got a package," his mom announced as she stuffed a lunch bag with a sandwich, an apple, some cookies, yogurt, beef jerky, and nuts. He remembered his own packed meals fondly and missed them when he'd had to scrounge for protein in the desert.

"A package for me?" Odd since he'd not ordered anything.

"I left it on the front hall table."

He moved to the space and noticed the bubble envelope. The neatly printed label addressed to him. No return address.

Odd.

Suspicious.

Could it be dangerous?

He headed outside with it before he started palpating it. He'd seen how small bombs could be and knew there were deadly threats out there that were no bigger than a few grains of dust.

But who would want to kill him?

A shake and a grope didn't tell him shit, other than it was flexible. He tossed it to the ground and covered his face.

It didn't explode. He crouched in the yard and pulled out a pocketknife to slice along an edge.

He pried open the envelope to see a baggie with something green inside.

Weed?

Who the fuck would mail him weed?

His lips pressed tight.

Tyson.

The little bugger must have used his ID to order some online. After all, it was legal now in Canada.

He tucked it back into the bubble envelope. He'd be having a talk with the boy after school. Time to get all big brother on Tyson's ass. Only dopes did drugs.

Dominick didn't tell his mom because she didn't need the stress. Restless, he mowed the lawn around the farmhouse. Chopped some wood for the stove. Winter was coming. He fed the chickens, despite how they squawked and freaked every time he got near. The goats bleated. And their one horse lay down on the ground. Only the barn cats seemed to like him.

He kept himself busy because, despite all his applications, he didn't get a call to go in for an interview. By mid-afternoon, his pacing feet had him going for a jog, which, no surprise, led him to the grocery store.

He saw Anika right away, standing at a register, wearing her bright smock. It eased something within him to see her.

He caught her eye as he walked in. She arched a brow, and he took it as an invitation to saunter over and say hello since no one was waiting to be checked out.

"Hey."

"Back already for more junk food?"

Dominick almost told Anika the truth, that he'd come just so he could see her. But that sounded lame, so he had a choice: either buy more food they didn't need or—

"Came to apply for that job you were telling me about."

Her brows rose. "You, a stock boy?"

"Are you saying I can't do it?" He bristled.

"I would have expected, with your military background, you'd go after something a little more security-oriented with better pay."

He shrugged. "I've applied to a few places, but until they get back to me, a man's gotta work." Or he ended up in a grocery store lying his ass off to a woman he couldn't stop thinking about. And he'd tried. A few times in the shower, but his hand couldn't compare.

"Darryl is the manager on duty if you want to talk to him." She pointed and then ignored Dominick as she greeted a person pushing a cart. Dismissed.

He took it less as an insult and more as the fact that she wanted to do her job.

Dominick headed in the direction she'd pointed to find the same twerp as the day before. The guy didn't look happy at his approach.

"You Darryl, the manager?"

"Yeah. Can I help you?" The kid's gaze narrowed suspiciously.

"I need a job."

Incredulity raised the pitch of the queried, "You want to work here?"

"Is that a problem?" Dominick asked.

"After what I saw yesterday, you don't seem like you'd be the right fit."

Don't hit the kid. Don't hit the kid. "Why is that, Darryl? Because I'm a veteran? You got a problem with the folks who protect this country? I'm sorry if my uncouth behavior annoys you. I learned it when I was serving in the military." He dropped his voice. "Saving you, Darryl."

"Thank you?" Squeaked out.

"Yes, you can thank me by doing one simple thing, Darryl. I hear you have a job opening to stock shelves, correct?"

A nod.

"Good. I'll start now, but I am not wearing a smock." Dominick did have a shred of dignity left.

"Stock boys wear T-shirts with the store logo."

"Fine."

Of course the store didn't have any in stock for someone Dominick's size. The large shirt hugged his upper body in a way that had some of the shoppers ogling and whispering. He heard giggles, too.

He ignored them. The one woman he wanted

interested in him continued to ignore him. And it wasn't for lack of trying to grab her attention. He chose to stock the shelves closest to the registers, baring his teeth at the boys in the back who thought to protest. They didn't argue long when he slung heavy boxes onto their carts and sent them to the more obscure aisles.

Dominick was a man on a mission.

One of seduction. Though he might need help. Only he couldn't bear to ask Stefan. Pompous prick. Surely, he could figure out how not to be an asshole when he talked to Anika.

Don't treat her like a sex object, even if he wanted to bury his face between her thighs.

No saying things that would make her hit him.

Compliment her on something other than the way her full hips made him want to grind against her.

The manager left around eight p.m., leaving only a few employees in the store and a handful of browsing customers.

Mission clock? Less than an hour to set his plot in motion.

At nine, the store would close, and that was when he'd suggest they go for a coffee at the Tim Horton's in the plaza. He'd show Anika that he could talk without making her angry, and she'd agree to a second date. And then a third.

Never mind why he wanted to date her. He had to do something. She'd been on his mind non-stop since their first encounter.

What if the coffee went poorly and she made an excuse to ditch him and she never agreed to see him again?

Maybe he wasn't ready. Should he wait?

Ding.

Every time the door slid open to the store, it chimed, letting the cashiers know that someone had entered.

Given it was close to closing time, he wondered what asshole decided they needed groceries last-minute.

As Dominick put the last case of tomato cans on the shelf, he heard it—faint arguing. He ambled up the aisle to the front of the store.

"—go away, Thomas."

"You can't tell me to leave. I've got a right to shop wherever I like."

"Not according to the restraining order. You're supposed to keep away."

"You going to call the cops? Go ahead. I'll tell them I didn't know you worked here. Honest mistake."

"We both know that's a lie."

"Is it? What you gonna do? Hit me. You know you want to."

"You'd like that, wouldn't you? Because then you could run to the cops and file another false report."

"You want it to stop? Then you know what to do."

"You are such an asshole." Her tone was low and angry, much more controlled than Dominick, who felt rage flaring within.

He strode from the aisle and growled, "Is there a problem?"

"Mind your fucking business." The guy, tall but reed-thin, didn't even turn around.

"It is my business, twatwaffle, when you're being a dickhead to someone I work with." He noticed relief in Anika's eyes as he neared.

The guy whirled, showing a thin face, a mean curve to his lips, and the kind of attitude that would have gotten his teeth knocked out if he were in the military. Dominick would be more than happy to show him how they did things in the ranks.

"I said fuck off. Anika and I go way back. Used to be married until the ungrateful cunt kicked me to the curb."

Married to this douchebag? "Sounds more like she finally got smart and threw out the trash," Dominick mocked.

The twerp didn't like it and drew himself up to his full height, a hint taller than Dominick, but he'd wager not as mean. "I'm having a private conversation, so butt the fuck out."

Rather than reply to the guy, Dominick looked at Anika. "You want to talk to him?"

She pressed her lips tight.

He frowned, whereas Thomas chuckled. "She knows better than to piss me off."

"Just go away, Thomas." Spoken without the fire Dominick had already gotten used to.

What kind of shit had this douchebag put her through that she wouldn't fight?

"Would you look at that? Nine o'clock, which means store-closing time. Let's go, you knuckle-dragging twat." Dominick didn't wait for the idiot to argue. He reached for Thomas's arm and twisted it behind his back.

"Ow. Let me go, asshole. This is assault."

Dominick frog-marched him and whispered softly, "Assault would be me rearranging your face permanently." As they reached the door, he shoved the guy out and watched him stumble. "Stay away from Anika."

"I'm going to have you charged," blustered Thomas.

"Go ahead. File charges. I guarantee it never goes to trial because they'll never find your body." He hoped his smile conveyed his seriousness.

The asshole gave him the finger. "You want the whore, keep her. She was a dud in the sack."

"More like your dick was probably too small to satisfy. Maybe you should stick to inflatable girl-friends. They might not be as disappointed."

The barb had the guy snarling as he stalked off. Pity. Had he stuck around, maybe Dominick could have goaded him into throwing the first punch. Then he could have legitimately knocked him out.

As Dominick returned to Anika, he caught her chewing her lower lip. He'd be more than willing to save her the trouble and bite it for her—along with other parts.

"Thanks." Grudgingly said.

"I'm surprised you didn't knock him out."

"I can't. Last time I did, it cost me."

"Fucker sued you?"

She nodded. "He does shit on purpose to taunt me into losing my temper so he can milk me for more money."

"Will you hit me if I say I don't know how you ever married the guy?"

She rolled her shoulders. "He wasn't always a dick. At least, not to my face. I should never have married him, but we had an accident when we were dating. I got pregnant."

"Shit, you're a mom?" He'd never have guessed.

She shook her head. "I lost the baby. But by then, we'd already gotten hitched because Thomas was determined that we not have a bastard. I tried to make it work for a while, but it got to the point where every time my phone rang, or someone knocked on the door, I was hoping it was someone coming to tell me he'd died in an accident. Before I started plotting his death myself, I asked for a divorce."

"He doesn't appear to have taken it well."

"That scum-sucking bastard took everything I had and then some," she huffed. "I've been trying to rebuild my life since, but he just won't leave me alone."

At her vehement statement, Dominick really wanted to chase after the fucker and beat the living crap out of him. Maybe dangle him from a tree and use him as bait for the wildlife. Pity he couldn't get a hold of those ants he'd encountered from his time spent in that prison camp.

"If you ever need a hand dealing with him, I'd be more than happy."

She shook her head. "This is my problem."

For now. She didn't know it, but it'd just become Dom's, too.

"You look a little wound up. How about we go for a coffee and talk?" Said more gruffly than intended. Probably too soon.

She'd say no for sure.

He'd ruined his chance.

The longer she eyed him without replying, the more he braced himself. When her mouth opened, he expected her to say no, to give him an excuse.

Instead, she knocked him flat when she said, "Sure. Why don't we go to my place and save ourselves the outrageous prices?"

8

Anika should have said no. Could have. Would have.

But the encounter with Thomas had left her simmering. Angry. And feeling a bit spiteful, too.

So she invited Dominick to her place, not sure what would happen.

Oh, for fuck's sake. She knew what she wanted to happen, and Dominick was handy. She'd fuck him and send him on his way.

He didn't reply immediately, and shame started heating within her. He must think her a whore. Or crazy, given she'd been giving him the cold shoulder.

"Are you sure?"

It surprised her that he'd asked. "Are you planning to kill me?"

"No!"

"Then, yes, I'm sure." Had he been a pig about it, she would have probably changed her mind, but he seemed genuinely shocked.

He didn't say much as he got into her car.

What was there to say? The wrong word might wake her to the insanity of what she did. She had to fill the void, though. "How did you like your first day of work?"

He uttered a choked laugh. "Okay, I guess. I mean, easy enough. Boring."

"If it's so boring, then why did you ask for the job?"

He glanced at her. "Because I wanted to be closer to you."

Said every stalker in the world. What did it say about her that it gave her a cheap thrill?

"I still don't like you." She stared straight ahead.

"If it helps, my feelings toward you are complicated. Hell, my whole *life* is complicated."

"Then why ask me out?"

"For the same reason I got a job at the store. I want to be around you."

That had her snorting. "You just met me yesterday."

"But I've known you longer."

"I hadn't seen you since high school," she pointed out.

"True, but did you know I crushed on you for months before graduation?"

The claim drew her gaze. "Why? I hit you and told you to jump off a bridge."

He shrugged. "What can I say? I liked that you said no."

The excuse caused her to snort. "So, in other words, if I'd said yes back then, you'd have lost interest?"

He leaned closer to say, "If you'd have said yes, we would have made out, and you'd have become my girlfriend."

"Until you went into the military."

He shrugged. "Probably. I didn't have the grades for college, and I wasn't interested in anything else at the time."

"What about now? And don't tell me you plan to be a stock boy for life."

"I don't know. My brother Stefan works the bar scene, which I hate. Raymond is some techno-geek. They've both offered to help me find something, but..." He shrugged. "None of it interests me."

"What do you like?" she asked him, more interested in his reply than expected.

"I liked the military."

"Then why leave?"

He went silent.

"That bad, huh?"

He huffed a breath. "Yes, and no. I started having episodes. Blackouts. They claimed PTSD and medically discharged me."

"You don't sound like you believe the diagnosis."

"Because despite all the wars and the things I did"—he rolled his shoulders—"it honestly didn't bother me. And my nightmares weren't about the missions."

"What do you have nightmares about?" This was the most he'd talked, and she found herself curious to know more.

"I dream about not being myself."

"Who are you?"

"Not who. What." He laughed. "I dream I'm a fucking jungle cat of all things. Which is why they thought I was crazy. For a while, I was convinced I had something living inside me."

"And now?" she asked.

"Now, I still feel as if my body is too small. When it gets to be too much, I jog."

She pulled into the spot for her apartment, the basement of a converted house. She paused, wondering if she should have driven them to a motel, only she didn't have that kind of cash. And really, best let him see the real truth of her life.

Maybe he'd save them the bother and run.

He got out, and while he glanced around, he said nothing.

They entered her apartment, and she felt shame for a moment. Embarrassment at its shabbiness. But it was clean. She might be poor, but you could damned well eat off her floor.

He didn't say anything disparaging. Nor did his expression convey any kind of disgust.

He pointed to her kitchen. "How about I get a pot of coffee started while you change?"

Did he seriously still think this invitation to her place was about coffee?

Since he apparently needed a stronger hint, she grabbed him by the shirt and mashed her mouth to his.

For a moment, he stilled, frozen against her.

"What's happening?" he asked.

"Sex, if you'd ever shut up."

"But—"

She slid him some tongue before she changed her mind.

He got the hint and kissed her back, his mouth hard and insistent against hers.

Passion erupted, the kind that soon had them panting against each other. Sucking at tongues. Biting at lips.

She had a bed, but they didn't make it to the bedroom. His hands spanned her waist, and he lifted her until her ass hit the Formica. Her knees spread to accommodate his body. With her new spot on the counter, he had to bend a bit to keep kissing her. Not that he had a choice given the way she had her hands clamped around his neck.

As their harsh breaths mingled, her pulse raced, and her pussy throbbed. She wanted this more than expected.

He dragged his mouth from her lips to her jaw then drew them over to the lobe of her ear. Tugging it. Sucking it. She uttered a mewling cry, and he growled against her, the sound making her shudder with need.

His mouth returned to crush hers, nipping and sucking, driving her crazy with passion.

She clung to him, her legs around his waist drawing him against her. She could feel him. Hard and ready.

Wanting her.

Just like she wanted him.

She tugged at his shirt and shoved it up, baring his flesh to her touch. Not just her fingers, though. She kissed his chest. Dug her nails into his skin once he removed the shirt. She licked around his nipples and felt a thrill at his low groan.

He wasn't content to just let her play.

His hands, big and callused, removed her shirt and then traced over her ribcage, drawing shivers of pleasure. He grumbled when her bra gave him trouble, but he managed to undo the clasp. The moment he freed her breasts, he cupped them, his thumbs stroking over the taut peaks. She leaned back, and he took the invitation. He dipped his head and claimed one of her buds.

His hot and wet mouth sucked and tugged at her nipples, pulling at them with his lips. He bit them lightly enough to draw gasps. He swirled his tongue around the buds before sucking them.

She held him by the belt loops and used her leverage to grind against him as he played with her nipples.

Arousal rode her hard, more than she imagined. Almost enough to be frightening, and yet, at the same time, she couldn't stop.

Wouldn't.

She wanted what he offered.

Needed to feel desired. Wanted pleasure.

His mouth left her breasts to blaze a trail down her stomach to the waistband of her pants. She throbbed, and yet he paused.

A glance through heavy-lidded eyes showed him peering at her.

She managed a husky, "What are you waiting for?"

He groaned, the sound reaching her through the fabric of her pants as he put his mouth on her.

Jesus, the heat. She moaned. Trembled. Then cried out as he blew even more hotly.

"Dom." She whispered his name, and it had him in a frenzy, his hands tugging at her pants. She heard fabric tearing as he managed to get them down.

"Fuck me, you smell so good." He growled just before his mouth pressed against her sex.

She cried out and arched, would have slid off the counter if not for his hands.

He held her safe so that he might pleasure her, his tongue swiping across her pussy. Lapping at her cleft. Parting her lips to jab at her core.

Her fingers scrabbled for purchase on the counter as her hips rocked in time to his licking. He held her spread wide and where he wanted so he could feast.

But he didn't just play with her clit. He suddenly fingered her. His rough finger penetrating and drawing a raw cry as she arched into his thrust.

He kept lapping at her clit as he slid a second finger in to stretch her, the digit long enough to reach that spot inside.

Stroke it.

Push at it.

Licking.

Thrusting.

Desire coiled. She panted as she reached the edge.

And then he growled against her, "Come for me, Annie."

Her orgasm exploded, a tensing spasm that hit her whole body and emerged on a scream.

She pulsed around his fingers, and he hummed in satisfaction against her, drawing it out until she whimpered.

"Too much."

He stood and dragged her close for a kiss where she could taste herself. But she didn't care. She throbbed. Pulsed. And she knew he did, as well.

She tugged at his belt then his pants. Reaching in to grab him, she heard him hiss.

Just as she was about to ask for a condom, his phone went off, the ring of it an insistent distraction.

He ignored it as he kissed her. She rubbed her thumb over his tip and said, "You got prot—?"

Dring. Dring.

His phone went off again, and he cursed. "Fuck me, why now?"

"I guess you better answer." She released him as the moment shattered.

He looked wild, passion still in his gaze, the slight hint of a pout on his lips. "I don't want to fucking answer. I want to be inside you."

She wanted it, too.

The phone stopped ringing but just as quickly started again.

He sighed. And then sighed again as he pulled it from his pocket and answered.

She didn't hear anything but saw his expression as it went from smoldering to cold and hard. He hung up and growled, "I gotta go."

"Oh." The word sounded more dejected than she liked, and to her surprise, he drew her close for a deep kiss and a grumbled, "Not leaving 'cause I want to, Annie."

Annie. She liked the way he softened her name.

"Need a ride?" she asked.

"No. My brother is coming to grab me."

"How does he know you're here?" She'd not heard him give an address.

The furrow in his brow matched his curled lip. "Fucker tracked my phone."

"Is everything okay?"

"My little brother is missing. And I gotta help find him." He dragged her to him and gave her another fierce kiss. "I will see you tomorrow."

He would?

For once, she didn't argue.

"Fuck me, this sucks," he grumbled as he left.

Whereas she touched her lips.

What had just happened?

The best sex of her life with a guy who usually said the stupidest things with his mouth. But he sure knew how to talk to her pussy.

9

Stefan was the one to pick him up. With it being just the two of them, Dominick could ask better questions.

"Why does Mom think Tyson is missing?"

"Because he might be mouthy, but he's always home by his nine o'clock curfew on school nights."

"It's only ten p.m."

"You want to repeat that to Mom?" was Stefan's wry reply.

Dominick grimaced. "Any ideas where he's gone?"

"Raymond tracked his phone to a spot in the woods. It's not moving."

"Doesn't mean shit. Could be he's out there drinking, or he's with a girl."

Stefan slanted him a look. "Is this your way of

trying to get out of searching? Because if you want, I'll turn around and drop you off."

"No." But he didn't say it in a happy tone. His gut said that Tyson was in trouble, and he knew better than to ignore it. It'd never steered him wrong, although it should be noted that it currently steered him in Anika's direction. He wanted her something fierce. Would have gladly gone back to her arms but for one thing.

Mom.

"What time did little bro leave the house?" Dominick asked to get a better sense of what might have happened.

"Sometimes before nine. According to Mom, he came down for a snack. She went up to bed to read. Noticed that he wasn't in his room when she went down to make sure everything was locked up."

More like she waited for Dominick. She didn't like to go to sleep until her babies were home.

"Is he a drinker?" Dominick had to ask. He'd not spent much time here in the last few years. Not enough to know, at any rate.

Stefan shook his head. "A few beers. Mostly to fit in, I think. But I have caught him smoking weed."

Dominick slapped the dashboard. "Little fucker. That would explain the package I got, then. Someone mailed an anonymous bag of green to me."

"No shit." Stefan breathed the words. "Is it any good?"

"How would I know? I don't do drugs." Not since the blackouts.

"Maybe you should. You might lighten up," Stefan observed.

"I'm fine. I don't need to get high." Didn't need to wake up with blood on his chin again. Because it wasn't enough that he'd had one episode. When they took him off active duty, he'd smoked another from that stash and woke up in the local market, amidst a pile of fish.

"If you say so. How's Anika?"

Heat warmed his face, and he shifted in the passenger seat. "She's good."

"Uh-huh," was all Stefan said, and yet it bugged Dominick.

"Stay away from her."

"Marking your territory?" His brother smirked at him. "Not to worry. Even I have some scruples."

Remorse hit him as he realized that he'd implied his brother would betray him that way. Stefan was many things but never a hurtful bastard to his family.

"Sorry. Something about her drives me a little batty."

"Isn't she the same girl you crushed on in high school?"

"You remember that?" He winced. Had he been that obvious?

"You had her picture ripped out of the yearbook by your nightstand."

Embarrassment had his face hot and ready to explode. "So what if I liked her?"

"Liked? You were obsessed. If you hadn't gone into the army, I have no doubt that she'd have had you arrested for stalking."

Dominick grimaced. "I don't understand what it is about her that makes me act like a jerk."

"Must have been love at first sight," Stefan mocked.

Love? Never.

They pulled into the driveway for their house and spilled out of the car. Mom was on the porch, arms wrapped around herself.

"Dominick, thank God. You have to find your brother." She seemed a little frantic.

"I'm sure he's fine. The boy's probably tripping in the woods. It's a guy thing. Remember when I did it?" He'd found some mushrooms. The magic kind. Spent a night thinking he was a giant cat, hunting in the woods.

"I do recall, and it was just as frightening," she yelled. "So don't remind me!"

His brows rose. "Sorry."

"Don't apologize. Find your brother!" Mom had gone past the point of scared into panic.

He hated seeing her like this, which was why he folded her into his arms and murmured, "Don't worry. We'll find him."

And then he was going to beat the crap out of his brother for scaring Mom.

"Which way?" he asked Stefan.

"In the woods, past the bridge over the creek, at least according to Ray."

"Where is Ray?" He didn't see his other brother often, as he spent most of his time in the basement.

"He's got some drones in the air, scanning for Tyson."

Well, shit. That would be helpful.

With a direction, Dominick loped across the field, headed for the woods. The same forest where Pammy had almost lost a leg because of a trap. An animal trap. Someone poaching on their land.

Despite installing hunt cams in the area around the metal jaws, which they'd replaced, minus the spring to launch them, they'd yet to capture the culprit.

And now, Tyson wandered in that same expanse of trees. A teen oblivious to the dangers. Perhaps injured. What if he'd had a blackout episode like Dominick did? Some drugs could make people do stupid shit—like think they could fly or breathe underwater.

No wonder his mom freaked. Was this how she'd felt each time he'd done something stupid? As it occurred to him just how bad this could be, Dominick moved faster, more worried than he would have ever admitted out loud.

Shit, he must be getting old.

The path in the woods, worn bare of weeds by regular walks, was barely visible. The moon was only a crescent. He saw well enough to navigate, long strides eating up the ground, his brother only a step behind him.

When his phone rang, he pulled it out with one hand and kept moving. "Yup."

Raymond was on the line. "Keep on the path. The last known location of his phone is by the creek where it splits."

"We gonna talk about the fact you've hacked our location services on our phones?" he asked.

"Nope." Ray kept his reply short.

"It's illegal."

"Yup."

"You ain't gonna stop, are you?" he asked.

"Nope." Ray didn't apologize.

"Have the drones seen anything?" Those little mechanical fuckers had saved a lot of lives when he was on missions. They could discern traps and locate items of interest, saving time while hunting.

"Forget the drones."

"Stefan said you deployed a pair."

"I did. One got taken out by a bird, and the other malfunctioned," Raymond groused.

"Poor Ray, lost his toys," Dominick taunted. His brother always did like electronics more than people.

Rather than reply, Raymond counted down. "Reaching the spot in five, four, three…"

A pace and then another before he stumbled to a halt.

"Fuck," Stefan muttered what he thought.

They'd found the phone, amidst the shreds of his brother's clothes. The shirt stretched and clawed. Pants and boxers on the ground. Shoes, too.

And beside it all, a familiar green baggie, along with a package of rolling papers.

10

"HE'S FUCKING TRIPPING IN THE WOODS," Dominick bellowed. "That fucking moron. I am going to throttle him."

"Shut up. If Tyson hears you, he'll hide. And if he hides, we can't go home to our nice comfy beds." Mom would kill them if they left Tyson out overnight.

Dominick wasn't done bitching, though. "Even if we find him, we can't bring him home, not while he's higher than those dudes who lick those frogs. Daphne shouldn't be seeing that kind of shit." Someone had to look out for his littlest sister.

Stefan rolled his eyes. "You do know that Daffy plays war games online?"

"What? Shouldn't she have like dolls or makeup or a playhouse or something?"

His brother winced. "How have you lived this long around women and not been murdered for the shit you say?"

Dominick pursed his lips. "Most of them haven't understood a word I've said." It made things easier. Talking led to him putting his foot in it. Just ask Anika.

Raymond was still on the phone, and he interjected. "Hello, shouldn't you be finding our little brother?"

That brought a deep sigh. "This is so not how I wanted this evening to end."

Yet it did, with him walking the woods, in the dark, the baggie of weed in his pocket. Just how potent could it be? Marijuana usually gave a mellow buzz. It calmed him, which was why he used to smoke it. But it took only one bad batch for him to quit. Could it be that Tyson got hit by the same kind of crap?

He pulled the bag free and sniffed it.

Something tickled his nose. Barely enough to notice.

He unsealed the bag, and the nicest aroma rose from it. He stuck his nose right in for a deeper whiff.

Smiled.

It didn't smell like weed, more like the most delicious thing in the world. He could have rolled in the stuff. It made him feel so good.

Rawr.

He shook his head as a noise burst from him. Startling, but not enough to distract from all the scents around him.

How had he not noticed the various aroma trails before? He turned his head left and right, tracing smells to their origin. Tree. Bush. Leaf. Poop.

Tyson.

More poop.

Wait, Tyson?

He pivoted to where he smelled it, something that reminded him of his brother. He followed, weaving through the trees, each deep breath diminishing the scent. Removing his warm glow.

The rumbling discontent within returned full force.

Without questioning if it was a good idea, he stuck his head in the dope bag for another sniff.

Instant feel-good and a languorous, loose-limbed sensation. His deciphering of smells sharpened, and he loped after Tyson's scent until it stopped at the base of a tree.

He glanced upward.

Way up.

Amidst the branches, he saw eyes glinting at him.

"Tyson?"

The reply was a growl, more animal than teenage boy.

"Stop fucking around and come down."

"Raw-rr." Another rumble of sound, and he began to wonder if perhaps it wasn't his brother.

Or could it be that Tyson tripped so hard he couldn't remember how to speak? He'd known guys in the military who'd gone on some wild hallucinogenic rides. Just look at Dominick, who remembered nothing of the last two times he'd smoked dope.

"Are you my brother or not?" He eyed the tree and then the branches. Sighed. He hated climbing. For a second, he considered taking another whiff but thought better of it.

He leapt for the lowest branch and grabbed hold, swinging his legs up to then flip and straddle it.

It wasn't until he stood, close to the trunk to grab another higher limb, that the thing above growled.

Low and rumbly. It didn't resemble his brother one bit, and yet the scent didn't lie. Faint, but unmistakable. Dominick always had a thing about pegging people by their smell.

Mom was a mixture of raspberry and honey. Stefan, pine trees in winter. Tyson had a hint of cinnamon with vanilla.

He moved up another branch then another. It sent the thing above scrambling, moving higher.

But just when he thought he had it cornered, it leapt to a different tree.

"Fucker."

It took him a while to climb back down. By the time he did, whatever he'd chased was gone.

He eyed the bag of dope and thought about seeing if he could find it again. Better not, because if that was Tyson, the green shit had obviously severely messed him up.

Rather than chase, he retraced his steps to the creek and the clothes. He kept his pace slow. Took plenty of breaks. Sensed he wasn't alone but never turned to look behind him.

He one-hand-texted his brother. *Stay away from the fork. Think he's following me.* He thumbed off the sound lest he startle the follower.

At the creek with the ruined clothes, he sat down, his back against a tree, and waited.

Heard the wind lightly whistling through the branches. The soft burble of the creek. The barely heard crack of a step on loose debris.

It took a long while before it got close enough for him to hear breathing. Short huffs.

He kept his eyes closed, hands on his thighs, sitting lotus-style—a relaxation technique taught by one of his shrinks.

It didn't relax him, but it helped him focus when he needed to have patience.

Like now. A body settled over his lap, smelling of Tyson but…something about it felt wrong.

He placed his hand on fur.

What the fuck?

11

AS HE JUMPED, THE FURRY BODY LEAPT FROM his lap. Dominick reached for his knife, wishing he'd brought a gun. The beast hit the ground and rolled. The area grew dark as a cloud crossed over the moon, meaning he couldn't see, but Dominick could hear.

A yowl and then a yell.

"Ow. Fuck. What the hell?" Despite the gloom, his brother's shape became suddenly distinct, on his hands and knees, head hanging, naked as the day he was born.

Dominick must have been sleeping and imagined the fur because that was most definitely Tyson.

His about-to-be-severely-grounded brother.

"You!" Dominick pointed. "You worried Mom by disappearing."

His brother turned a wan face in his direction. "What happened?"

"Don't play dumb. I know you went into my room and stole those drugs you had mailed to the house in my name."

"What?" Tyson rocked back on his heels and noticed his nudity. "Where are my clothes?"

Dominick pointed. "On the ground. Where you left them. When you got high!"

With each punctuated statement, Tyson winced. "I thought it was weed."

"What do you mean *thought*? You ordered it."

Tyson shook his head. "Nah. That shit isn't mine. I usually get it from a guy at school."

"How did you know I had it then?" Because he'd hidden it under his pillow.

"Found it when I stripped your bed for Mom."

"And stole it!"

"Borrowed," Tyson corrected. "I meant to put it back before you got home from work, but..." Tyson looked down. "Guess I smoked a little too much and lost track of time."

"You think?" Fuck going soft on him. The boy needed to learn a lesson.

"I'm sorry," was his choked whisper.

"You will be. Because you do know you made Mom cry."

Tyson cried, too, when he was reunited with her. She rushed from the house the minute Dominick brought his brother across the field.

Rather than follow them inside, he paused and waited for Stefan to join him.

"Where did you find him?" his brother asked.

"I didn't. He found me."

"Did he say what happened?"

"This." Dominick dangled the bag, and the overwhelming urge to sniff it almost snapped his control. "But he claims he wasn't the one to buy it."

Stefan lifted his hands. "Don't look at me. I'm a drinker and a cigarette smoker. I don't do drugs."

"Whatever it is, it's not pot." Dominick had no idea what it was other than delicious-smelling and potent. How else to explain his sensation in the woods that he was a mighty hunter able to discern scent like a dog.

"Maybe it's oregano," Stefan joked.

Could oregano make him imagine a huge cat in his lap instead of his brother?

"I doubt oregano made Tyson strip."

"You should give it to Raymond. He knows people who can analyze it. Maybe it's some new street drug."

Maybe.

Whatever it was, it had highly addictive attributes, which was why he was happy to hand it off to his brother. And then he went to bed.

After all, he was supposed to work in the morning.

He was fired by noon.

12

Anika woke the next morning and stretched. No alarm. No work today. Most people got weekends off. Anika got Wednesday and Friday. Which suited her just fine.

Dominick had said she'd see him today.

She hadn't yet decided what to do about him. Or what she thought about what'd happened.

Not being the type to indulge in casual affairs, she had no idea what last night meant.

Did it mean anything?

They'd exchanged no promises. On the contrary, she'd barely let him speak, mostly fearing he'd say something stupid.

Could she believe him when he said that he was drawn to her? As if she had the power to addle someone's wits. Still, there was something heady about a man like him admitting that he had a weakness for her.

And he was incredibly talented with his tongue.

She shivered deliciously and almost stayed in bed to masturbate. However, she didn't know when to expect him, which meant she spent the morning cleaning and switching out her sheets.

He didn't call.

Didn't show up.

A log in to the work portal online showed him slated to work until dinner. She spent the afternoon baking. Then she bathed, taking time to shave and pluck to the point her skin throbbed. It had been a while since she'd tended her garden.

Dinnertime came.

He didn't.

She ate alone. It was quite excellent. A raspberry walnut salad with a grilled chicken breast and riced cauliflower.

The evening ticked along. It would be an understatement to call herself disappointed.

She'd just resigned herself to spending it alone when a knock sounded at the door.

Her heart stopped beating.

He's here.

She smoothed her hair and took a deep breath.

With butterflies in her belly, she opened the door with a smile, only to gasp in shock.

"You're not supposed to be here."

Thomas shoved her inside and kicked the door shut. "Expecting your boyfriend?"

"I don't have a boyfriend."

"Lying whore. I saw him leave your place last night."

"You were spying on me?" Anika gasped.

"Fuck yeah, I was. Because I know you're holding out on me." His eyes had red streaks. His hair appeared unwashed. "Give me your cash."

"Are you insane? What cash? You took everything plus some."

"Where's the rest?"

"There is nothing else," she cried. "Now get out, or I'm calling the cops."

She moved for her phone on the kitchen counter, but he lunged for her. Grabbed her. Slammed her into the wall hard enough that her teeth clacked.

His gaze wild, Thomas snarled, "I need money."

"I have nothing. Leave me alone." She struggled in his grip. While he'd never hit her before, he didn't seem balanced tonight. His fingers dug into her arms, and she smelled alcohol on his breath.

"Where's your bank card? What's your code?"

Before she could tell him to go fuck himself, that he wasn't getting the eleven dollars and eighty-five cents in her account, there was another knock on her door.

Both their gazes slewed toward it.

"Annie, it's me."

Dominick.

Her lips parted, only to have Thomas slap a hand over her mouth as he shushed her.

She glared at him.

"Don't you fucking say a word," he breathed.

Like hell. She solidly bit him.

"Argh, you bitch." Releasing her mouth, he wound back his fist.

"Help!" she shrieked.

The door smashed open as Dominick entered.

Big. Bad. And pissed.

Thomas never managed to land the blow because Dom moved too fast. One second, he was kicking open her door. The next, he was tossing Thomas across the room.

Before her ex could get up, Dom had stalked over and hauled him up by the shirt. Brought his face close and said, "Do you want to die?"

"You can't threaten me," Thomas gasped.

"Actually, I fucking can, you coward. Going after a woman." Dom shook him. "Let me make this clear for you. If you come anywhere near Annie again, you will die."

"Hurt me, and I'll have you arrested," Thomas choked.

"I won't hurt you because I don't have to. I hear

the Mason brothers are looking for the person who stole their shipment."

"I don't know what you're talking about."

Dom's smile was cold as he said, "Feel free to tell them that when they're torturing you for its location."

Thomas's eyes widened. "You can't fucking blackmail me."

"Yeah, I can. So, you decide. Is harassing your ex-wife more important than your fingers and toes? How attached are you to your kneecaps?"

"You want her. Have at her. She's trash," Thomas spat.

"More like the treasure you didn't recognize, asshole. Out." Dominick dragged Thomas to the door and literally tossed him out. He then did his best to close the door, only the busted jamb proved problematic.

"Oh, shit. Sorry I broke it."

"Don't be." She'd never been so happy to see someone. She hated how easily Thomas had disarmed her. How she forgot to fight because of her fear that he'd take even more from her than he already had.

But Dominick wasn't afraid.

"I want to kill him for real," he muttered as he knelt to inspect the damage.

"I wouldn't complain. Hell, I'd give you an alibi."

She winked.

His smile was grim as he said, "I might take you up on that. But until that time, I need a tool kit. A hammer, preferably."

"Okay. But I warn you, it's pink."

It was also child-sized, according to him. He worked quietly fixing the door; meaning she got to watch.

He really was a nicely put-together man. And while dour of expression most of the time, it made the way he softened in her presence all the more special and attractive.

When Dom was satisfied with the door repairs, he closed and locked it. Only then did he finally face her.

"Sorry I was late getting here. I went to the store first."

"It was my day off."

"Which would have been useful to know," he grumbled.

"You could have easily checked the schedule at the store."

"It's on the computer, and I'm not good with that shit. You'll have to tell me, and I'll try to remember."

"Why do you care about my hours?" Never act too eager. All the articles she'd ever read stated it like a golden rule. Hard to get. Aloof. Make him work for it. Don't just rip off the panties and yell at him to shut up and take you.

All conscious thought went out the window when he said, "I wish I'd known so I could have spent it with you."

For a second, warmth filled her. So sweet. And nice. And...then she understood why he'd shown up at all. "Are you here because you got interrupted? I should mention I'm not a believer in tit for tat. Last night, I was in the mood. Tonight, I'm tired..."

"Then we'll go to bed." He smiled wickedly.

"That wasn't what I was suggesting."

"Would you rather we made out on the couch?"

She lifted her chin. "I'm not a sex doll. Maybe I want to talk."

He collapsed onto her sofa and spread his arms across the top. "Okay. Talk about what?"

Well, damn, she'd not expected him to capitulate so easily. She scrambled. "Your brother. Did you find him?"

"I did."

"And?" she grumbled, sitting across from him in a hardback chair. Not as comfortable as a couch cushion or his lap.

"The little fucker thought it would be a bright idea to smoke some unknown substance. In the woods, by himself. He ended up having some hardcore hallucinations. He's lucky he didn't get hurt."

EVE LANGLAIS

"But he's okay?"

"Yeah. But he tripped pretty hard. Got naked and ran around for about an hour. Says he doesn't recall a single thing."

"What the heck did he smoke?"

"That's the weird thing. My brother Raymond, he's got connections, so he sent the baggie of dope to his buddy, who swears it's catnip."

"Catnip doesn't get people high." She wrinkled her nose.

"That's what I said. I should add I took a whiff of what was in that bag. It was definitely more than just catnip."

"Did you get stoned, too?" she asked.

"A bit. Yeah," he admitted.

"Okay, that's weird. I could have sworn I once read an article that said catnip didn't affect humans." A quick search on her phone only reinforced that truth.

Dom frowned. "That doesn't make sense because Ray's friends seemed pretty sure."

She tapped her lower lip and then said, "I've got an idea. Wait here a second."

It took her only a few minutes to knock on her neighbor's door, and then she was back with a spray bottle.

He eyed it. "What is that?"

"Catnip juice. Maureen, my upstairs neighbor,

has like four cats. Figured she might have some."
She spritzed it into the air and sniffed. Wrinkled her
nose. "Not exactly appetizing."

And yet, even as she said it, he'd slunk off the
couch and was on his knees in front of her, eyes
closed, face lifted.

"What are you talking about? That smell... Fuck
me, that's good."

It was weird how he softened and yet hardened at
the same time. She sprayed the air again, and he
caught it with his skin and breathed deeply then
released the air in a low rumble.

When he opened his eyes, there was a wildness
in their depths.

"Annie." He purred her name.

"Are you okay?" she asked.

"Never better." He put his hands on her hips and
pressed his face to her groin. Blew hotly through her
pants. She gasped, her fingers curling in his hair.

He nipped at her through the fabric, and she
moaned. Swayed.

"Where's the bed?" Before she could answer, he'd
stood and lifted her into his arms.

He kissed her as he found the door to her
bedroom then laid her down gently.

Still kissing.

There was a sexiness to his actions, a reckless
abandon as he tugged off her shirt, growling in his

haste. Especially when it got caught and she had to help him.

Her breasts were encased in her good bra, put on in anticipation. She was glad she'd not changed out of it before his arrival.

He buried his face in the valley between her breasts and breathed hotly.

"Are you sure you're okay with this?"

Actually, it was probably a bad idea to sleep with him, but she didn't care. He drove her wild. Made her want.

Her turn to yank at his shirt, wanting to feel the firmness of his flesh against her. Their pants hit the floor in a frenzy that rid her of underwear, too.

There was none of the awkwardness that sometimes happened the first time all parties got fully naked. He was built like a brick house. Solid all over.

And he appeared to love her body. It wasn't just his hands worshipping her. His gaze smoldered. His dick...

It bobbed, hard and more than ready.

He cupped her pussy and growled. "Wet."

He moved until he could nuzzle her mound. She grabbed at his hair as she parted her thighs.

"Smell so good," he whispered against her nether lips.

His first lick was a slow, long swipe. She shuddered and sighed his name. "Dom."

He tongued her, making her flesh quiver. Her hips gyrated. She dug her nails into his scalp.

She cried out as the tip of his tongue flicked rapidly, teased back and forth against her clit.

So good.

So very, very good.

She gasped and writhed.

He kept stroking until she had her first orgasm. She cried out, and her back arched. The climax rippled through her, and still he licked. Until she began whimpering.

Needing.

"Dom." She moaned his name.

"Give me a sec," he growled. She heard the crinkle of plastic and, through lids heavy with passion, watched him put on the condom.

When he finally unrolled it, he caught her gaze and rumbled, "Mine."

Possessive and sexy.

Palming her ass cheeks, he dragged her to the edge of the bed and lifted her to the right height. He prodded her with his erect cock, rubbing the swollen head against her slick pussy. Teasing them both.

"Dom." His name emerged with a low, guttural sound this time.

He slid into her, and she arched. Breathing hitched, she felt him stretching her. Filling her. So perfect.

Her legs wrapped loosely around his waist, she let him control the pace. He held her firmly and pressed in and out of her with a slowness that was both excruciating and amazing.

He thrust, in and out, creating a delicious friction that suddenly turned into pressure as he drove deep and then proceeded to rotate only his hips, grinding into her.

Hitting her sweet spot.

Over and over.

Until her fingers clawed at his shoulders.

Only when she screamed and came on his cock did he start thrusting again, drawing out the waves of her orgasm and then transcending it.

She'd never been pleasured to near death.

And it took a while for her to come back down to earth. To find herself cradled in his arms, spooned against him, his face in her hair.

Smart man, he didn't say a word. Just cuddled.

13

In the middle of the night, Dominick woke with a major thirst. Carefully, so as not to disturb Anika, he slipped out of bed, and padded quietly to the kitchen.

As he poured himself a glass of water from the tap, he noticed the stupid catnip fragrance bottle. Earlier, it took only a spritz for him to lose a bit of control and ravish Anika—not that he needed much encouragement.

Did it really affect him? Anika wasn't here to distract. He lifted the bottle to his nose and took a good whiff. Fucking amazing. No wonder felines loved it.

Before he could question his sanity, he poured some—all—into his glass of water and carried it to the window, where he peeked out. This time of night, the neighborhood lay dormant, the street-lights illuminating empty sidewalks.

Almost empty.

He saw the bright flare of a cigarette. Someone outside having a smoke. No big deal. He took a swig of his water.

Mmm. Nice.

The person with the smoke shifted, and their face came into view.

What the fuck? It was that asshole, Thomas.

He took another swig then another, downing the whole glass before heading outside, realizing only as the cool air hit him that he was still naked.

He didn't care. When Thomas opened his mouth to say, "What the fuck?" it seemed only natural to snarl. Then he gave chase to the running man.

DOMINICK WOKE CURLED AROUND ANIKA. Content. Warm. A good place to be, considering his strange dream. He'd dreamt that he hunted, his prey fleet of foot, but not as fast as him.

Anika stirred, and he slid his hand from her bare hip to her mound. He palmed her, and she uttered a soft sigh and rolled her hips against him.

"You awake?" he whispered against her hair.

"Barely."

"I've got something to help with that." He parted

her thighs, slipping his finger in enough to stroke her, finding her wet already.

She moaned as he replaced his hand with his cock, his arm around her waist, keeping her spooned against him as he rocked and thrust gently into her. When he felt himself getting close, his finger went to her clit and rubbed it. Rubbed until he felt that sweet pussy of hers clenching around him, drawing his own orgasm.

He held her as they cooled from their climax. Happy to spend the day in bed with her, but she wiggled.

"I need to shower."

"Sounds like an excellent plan."

She shot him a look over her bare shoulder as she sat up. "It's not big enough for two."

"Then I'll watch," was his reply, along with a wicked grin.

She blushed.

Fuck he was head over heels for this girl.

He watched her bathe. Then licked her until she came again. But when he would have dragged her back to bed, she shook her head.

"I can't. I work one to nine, which means I need to do my laundry this morning."

"I'll give you a hand."

"What? No."

But he wasn't taking no for an answer. "Is that

your basket?" He pointed.

"Yeah."

"Where's your machine?"

"I don't have one. I use a laundromat."

He grimaced. "Not today, you're not. We're going to my house."

"I am pretty sure your mom doesn't want me using her washer."

"Why not?"

"Because of the wear and tear on her machine along with electricity costs." She rolled her eyes as if it were obvious.

She didn't know his mom very well. "One, she really wouldn't give a shit. And two, if it makes you feel better, you can pay her the coins you would have used at the store."

"If you don't want to come to the laundromat, that's fine. I don't mind doing it alone."

He leaned close. "Never said I minded. If you really insist, we'll go to your laundromat, but my place might have cookies or brownies."

"Don't you have to work?" she asked.

"No." Then he added, "I might have gotten fired."

Her mouth rounded. "This is because of Thomas, isn't it?"

"Kind of. Apparently, he complained to the head office, and when the manager asked me not to threaten him again, I kind of said I couldn't make that promise."

Actually, his exact words were: *"If that mother-fucker shows up again to harass Anika, you might find his body in a dumpster with the garbage."*

"I'm sorry."

"Don't be. I'll find another job."

A knock at the door had her frowning. He tensed.

"I take it you're not expecting anyone?" he asked.

She shook her head.

"I'll answer."

She put her hand on his arm. "What if it's Thomas?"

The fear in her made him bristle. "It better not be that fucker." He flung open the door to find two cops standing on her doorstep.

"Can I help you?" Dominick asked, shirtless but wearing his pants. The female cop eyed him with cold appraisal, but the young guy smiled and winked.

"We're looking for Anika Mandelson."

"That's me. Can I help you?" Dominick could hear the dread in her voice.

"Do you know a Thomas Fitzpatrick?"

"Yeah. He's my ex-husband." Her lips turned down. "What has he complained about now?"

"When was the last time you saw him?"

"Last night. He showed up here asking for

money." She left out the part where Dominick arrived to find the fucker threatening her.

"And?" the cop with the badge that said *Ramirez* asked.

Anika's lips pursed. "There's nothing else to say. I said no. He left."

"What time did he leave?"

She shrugged and glanced at Dominick. "You arrived as he was going. Was that nine or ten?"

"Closer to ten," he supplied. "He left when I showed up."

"You are?" the female cop asked.

He puffed out his chest as he said, "Dominick Hubbard. Her boyfriend." He snaked an arm around her waist to draw her close.

Anika didn't protest. "What's this about, officers?"

"Mr. Fitzpatrick was attacked last night. Badly. He's currently in intensive care."

"What?" Then her eyes widened as she exclaimed, "It wasn't me." When Ramirez shifted her gaze to Dominick, Anika quickly added, "And it wasn't Dom. We stayed in all night."

"Can you provide proof?"

Dom leered slightly as he said, "How many recently used condoms would you accept as evidence?" Which reminded him. He'd forgotten one this morning—something to worry about later.

The cop pursed her lips. "Do you own a cat?"

"A cat?" She wrinkled her nose. "No. I'm more of a dog person, but Thomas took Jackson in the divorce."

"Are you sure, Ms. Mandelson? Because Mr. Fitzpatrick was quite adamant that you and your boyfriend released some kind of large cat from your apartment and it attacked him."

"Hold on a fucking second. That asshole tangled with an alley cat and got a few scratches, and you're blaming Anika?" Dominick couldn't hide his incredulity.

"It was larger than a domestic. The tears in his flesh are consistent with his claim that a panther attacked him."

Anika laughed. "Oh my God. You can't be serious. I don't know what Thomas's done this time, but I assure you, I don't keep exotic animals in my place."

"Then you won't mind if we have a look?"

She shook her head and stepped aside. "Be my guest."

Usually, Dominick would have advised against inviting questioning cops inside, but she had nothing to hide in this case.

The cops paced through the apartment, which didn't take long. Dominick and Anika remained in the kitchen, waiting for the coffee to brew, which was when he saw the bottle of catnip spray by the counter.

Empty. Because he'd drunk it. Weird. He blamed a shift in his taste buds from his time overseas. He dumped it into the garbage as he got them both a cup of coffee ready.

The police officers soon returned from searching the bedroom and bathroom to take a quick peek in the kitchen, barely large enough for two people.

Ramirez wasn't done. "Do any of your neighbors have pets?"

"Mrs. Hyde upstairs has a few cats, but the biggest, Floof, is old and blind in one eye. He's also not allowed outside. And he looks nothing like a panther, given he's white with a brown patch between his eyes."

"What about her other pets?"

"Small and also indoor cats."

"Thank you for your time, Ms. Mandelson. Please be aware, we might return with more questions."

"Perhaps instead of wasting time investigating my girlfriend, you should look into Thomas's associates. Rumor has it he has a gambling problem," Dominick stated. Or so Raymond had told him when he asked for a background check. He'd wanted to scout out potential problems.

The cops left, and Anika's shoulders slumped. "I swear it's never-ending drama with that man.

Accusing me of siccing a jungle cat on him? What the hell is that about?"

"Weird," Dominick agreed, but disturbing, too, because it reminded him of his dream.

A dream where he was a hunter, stalking prey, and that prey had Thomas's face.

He eyed the garbage can where he'd dumped the catnip spray. Why had he drunk it? And what happened after? Because he didn't remember going back to bed.

However, he did recollect washing his hands—clean of blood.

14

FRAZZLED BY THE COPS' VISIT, ANIKA DIDN'T argue when Dom insisted that they go to his place to do laundry. If he wanted to be bored out of his mind watching her sort, wash, and fold, then he could have at it.

She still couldn't figure out his interest in her.

Hell, she had a hard time figuring out her feelings about him but couldn't deny he made her feel amazing. Desired. Protected.

But at the same time, she wondered about him. She'd not mentioned the fact that she'd woken in the night and he wasn't in bed.

Then again, he wasn't a wild animal, so even if he'd gone out, he couldn't have been what attacked Thomas. And she didn't see him as the type to be so elaborate that he'd steal a panther from a zoo and set it free for the attack. Ottawa didn't even have a zoo, so chances were Thomas had lied.

"You're brooding," Dom remarked, his hand on her thigh as she drove.

She chewed her lip before blurting out, "I woke last night, and you were gone."

"I got thirsty."

"Oh."

"Anika." He said her name softly, and she cast him a quick glance. "While I don't like your ex, I didn't attack him. I wasn't kidding when I said he had a lot of enemies."

"I believe you. I just wish he'd leave me alone." She huffed out a tired breath.

He squeezed her leg. "Don't lose hope. Maybe this will be the wake-up call he needs to get out of town before his enemies decide to do worse next time."

"I should be so lucky," she grumbled.

As they reached the house, they noticed a dejected teenage boy sitting on the porch.

"Tyson, what are you doing here? Shouldn't you be in school?" Dominick asked, stepping out of her car. He'd yet to ask to drive, and while she shouldn't compare, she did with Thomas, who insisted that women sucked behind the wheel.

"Nana's taking me to the doctor to run some

tests. She wants to see if they can figure out what happened to me the other night."

"You got high. Don't need a physical or blood test to determine that."

Tyson shrugged. "She says she wants to make sure I didn't mess myself up."

"Doubtful. If catnip were dangerous, they wouldn't sell it in stores."

Maybe not dangerous, but no doubt Dom had gotten frisky after smelling some last night.

"She thinks it was laced with something," Tyson offered.

To which Dom replied, "Probably was, which is yet another reason your dumb ass shouldn't have smoked it. I still don't know what you were thinking, rolling a joint with some unknown substance. What if it was poison? You could have died."

"I know." A soft murmur as Tyson hung his head.

Mrs. Hubbard emerged, saying, "Are you ready to go?" Then, on a startled note, added, "Well, hello there again, Anika. So nice to see you."

"Hello, Mrs. Hubbard."

"Please, call me Nana."

"Okay," she agreed, even as it went against everything she'd been taught growing up. One did not call older adults by their first names.

"Oh, and before I forget, what are you doing for Thanksgiving?" Nana asked.

"Eating with us," Dom answered for her.

"I am?"

"Unless you have plans?" Nana queried.

She shook her head.

"Excellent. Bring an appetite, because I'm making a turducken this year, along with a ham and a beef roast."

"And tourtière!" Dom said, aiming for the trunk of Anika's car and pulling out her basket of dirty clothes.

"I swear you're obsessed with my meat pie." Said with fond exasperation.

"'Cause it's the best thing ever." Carrying her laundry, Dom passed his mom on the stairs. "I told Annie she could do her laundry here instead of at a laundromat."

"Dom insisted. I can take it into town," Anika hastily added.

"Don't be foolish. You shouldn't be washing your unmentionables with strangers."

"Thanks. I brought my own detergent," she said.

Mrs. Hubbard snorted. "You are way too polite. Dominick could learn a lesson or two from you."

"Don't worry, Mom. She's been teaching me all kinds of stuff." He winked at Anika, and she blushed.

His mom beamed. "You're staying for lunch?"

"I shouldn't. I've got to be at work for one."

"Well then, don't be shy in the kitchen. I've got

some goodies you can nibble on. Dom, make sure she's fed before she goes."

"How long you going to be gone?" Dom asked as he held open the door, waiting for Anika.

"At least an hour. Depends on how many tests they run."

As Tyson followed his mom to the sky-blue mini-van, he glanced over his shoulder and mouthed, *Save me.*

Dom smirked and then shouted, "You should tell them to check his prostate."

Tyson's eyes widened. Chuckling, Dom led the way into the house.

A little less frazzled this visit, she looked around a bit more than the previous time. Noticed the freshly painted walls and the vintage wooden floors with their light gleam. Pictures adorned the hallway wall, bearing different frames and the images of kids —Dom and his family growing up.

She paused in front of one with a gap-toothed boy with his foot resting on a soccer ball. "Is that you?"

He grinned. "Yup. Best on my team for a few years running until I broke my leg."

"Ouch. How did that happen?"

"Jumping off the barn into a hay bale."

She turned wide eyes on him. "That's dangerous."

"No shit. Especially when you miss."

The washer and dryer were in the mudroom off the kitchen, which meant walking through a heavenly smell. On the island, a tray of what looked like cinnamon rolls, drowning in icing, still liquid from being poured onto the hot treats.

"Ooh. My favorite." Dom moaned, almost in as much pleasure as he had in the shower that morning when she'd put her mouth on him. The throbbing between her legs approved of the fact that he found her more delicious than his treat.

He set the basket down and leaned over the goods, eyes closed in rapture as he inhaled. "Want one?"

"Sure."

He expertly slid a cinnamon bun, gooey with sticky sugar, onto a small plate, still warm to the touch. She held the edge of the plate to her mouth and tugged off a bite with her teeth.

She groaned, almost as loudly as when he'd had his face between her thighs.

"Dear God, that's good." She couldn't help but savor each delicious bite. When she finished it, she seriously debated licking the plate.

He didn't. His tongue made quick work of the icing, and she followed suit.

"That was insanely good," she said, following his example and placing the plate in the dishwasher.

"It was. But we need to pace ourselves. Laundry before another one."

"Another one?" She couldn't help the excited lilt.

"You are so fucking cute." He drew her to him for a kiss, nibbling her lips, making her melt. Given the pleasure, she kind of now wished she'd not been so hasty years ago. Sure, his methods might be crude, but damn, the man set her girly parts on fire.

And the magazines did claim you could teach a man new tricks. In her case, she could teach him the do's and don'ts of today's world.

He ended the embrace and with a gruff voice said, "We should probably get the laundry going before I take you on this counter and get into trouble with my mom."

How wrong was it that she wanted him to do exactly that?

The laundry room was a mudroom essentially with a door leading into the yard. However, add one big man into a super small space, and she couldn't help her awareness of him.

Dom watched as she measured out soap and dumped in her light clothes for the first load. Only once she got it going did he drag her into his arms for another kiss.

"Wanna sneak up the back stairs to my room?" he whispered against her mouth.

She did but... "What if someone hears us?"

"Raymond's probably in the basement. Don't worry, he won't bug us."

While tempted, she refused. "I can't. It's too weird for me."

He sighed. Sadly.

She laughed. "We could go for a walk instead." She'd noticed a trail going into the woods.

"Let's go." He dragged her to the door and opened it, only to exclaim, "Fuck!"

"What's wrong?" She peeked around him to see the world wet and cold. The rain cancelled the walk before it even began.

So much for it ending in sex.

The disappointment was real.

"I don't know about you, but I could use another cinnamon bun," he suggested.

"Yes!" She practically dragged him to the kitchen, as eager as he to have another.

Only to hear him yell, "No!"

To their shock, in the minutes they'd been gone, the pan had been emptied. Only traces of the icing were left behind.

Delicious when she swiped a finger across it and licked. She dragged a digit through the sugar trail again and held it to his lips.

He sucked it. Slowly. Erotically. Her toes curled as she rocked on her heels.

Mmm.

Maybe she should go with him upstairs.

"Dude, get a room."

She recoiled, backing away from Dom, moving abruptly enough she would have landed on the floor if not for his arm holding her in place.

Dom glared. "Great timing, Ray."

"Better me than Mom."

"Mom took Tyson to the doctor's and you know that, cockblocker."

Raymond smirked. "Yup."

"Did you eat all the cinnamon rolls, too?"

"You know I'm more of a protein guy."

"Maeve," he grumbled. "She's got radar for anything with cinnamon in it."

"You snooze, you lose." Raymond shrugged. "Listen, I didn't come upstairs just to wreck your sex life. I gotta show you something."

Sex life?

Oh, God.

The embarrassment tripled.

She tugged to move out of his arms, but Dominick held her firm.

"Does it have to be now?"

"Yes." Raymond shot her a look. Then added, "Alone."

Which was her cue. "I should check on my laundry."

It wasn't quite ready to swap, so she sat on the

washer and pulled out her phone, not that she had much to browse. She'd had to give up social media because of Thomas.

When Dom came to find her, he inserted himself between her legs, with his hands grasping

"Everything okay?" she asked.

"Yeah."

He didn't sound all right.

"What's wrong?"

"Nothing."

She frowned. "Bullshit." She wiggled to get off the washer.

"Where are you going?"

"Away from someone who lies to me." Because he was obviously disturbed.

He sighed. "Not lying, more like trying to process something really fucked up."

She arched a brow, nothing more.

He kept talking. "And you're right. If we're gonna be together, no secrets. Which I'm gonna say right now is hard for me. In the military, we're trained to not talk about shit."

"I'm not asking for military secrets. I want to know why you appear troubled." Because it bothered her.

"I'll explain, but we need to run an errand at the same time."

"Now?"

He nodded.

"But my laundry…" she protested.

"It will get done. I'll send Raymond a text to swap it."

Get another man to do her clothes? "I don't—"

He pulled her close and kissed her. That quieted her argument.

The embrace ended too soon, and he grabbed her hand to drag her after him.

"Where are we going?" she asked as they headed for her car.

"Pet store."

"What for?" she asked.

"Because I need catnip."

She paused. "Dare I ask why?" Then she added, "Is this about the catnip spray thing from last night?" She could have sworn it was still half-full, and yet this morning, she'd found it empty and in the trash.

"Raymond has this weird theory that Tyson might be allergic to it somehow. Or susceptible."

"Your brother isn't a cat."

"That's what I said. But"—he hung his head—"I have to wonder if Raymond is on to something. Because the baggie my brother smoked, just smelling it had me getting a little high."

"So, you're going to buy some more, and what? Smoke it?" She was only half joking.

128

"Possibly. Whatever helps Raymond and his tests."

"Is your brother some kind of scientist?"

"Of sorts. He's a hacker, who is also an information junkie."

Reaching her car, she pulled out her keys and said, "You drive."

"Me? Why?"

"So I can see if you're a road-raging maniac or that annoying twat who drives the speed limit or under."

"I don't suppose you'll give me a hint as to which one won't get me into trouble?"

She smiled. "Guess you'll find out."

She actually didn't care, so long as he didn't crash, which she planned to make difficult. Because the moment she was buckled in, her hand went to his thigh.

He rumbled, "You do realize we left a perfectly good bunk bed behind."

She blinked. "You invited me to your bunk bed?"

"Top mattress."

That brought a chuckle. "Maybe we should stick to sex at my place."

"If you insist. Personally, anywhere you are is a good spot to me."

She agreed. It made her bold. Her hand crept over

to his groin. "Earlier, you told the cops you were my boyfriend."

"Yup."

"You never officially asked me," she mentioned.

"I'd say it became obvious the first time my face was between your thighs and you came for me."

Heat filled her—all over. "What if I'm not looking for a relationship?"

"Too bad. You've got me now."

"You're bossy," she declared, giving him a squeeze. He was hard for her. Had been from the moment she put her hand on him. There was something powerful and erotic about his unabashed desire.

The car slowed.

"Why are we stopping?" she asked.

He turned to face her. "Anika, I know I'm a fucking dumbass most of the time and say the stupidest shit, but I like you. A lot. Mostly 'cause you put me in my place. You ain't afraid of me. And you're sexy as all fuck. Will you be my girlfriend?"

Not the most eloquent of speeches, but so utterly heartfelt she didn't just give his cock a squeeze through his pants; she unzipped him. Slipping out of the upper part of her seatbelt, she leaned over to put her face right above the bulge in his underwear.

"Um, Anika, we're kind of parked on the side of the road."

"Don't let anyone see me then," she advised before pulling him free.

Having been with a few guys, she knew he was only slightly more than average length but thick. So thick she had to stretch her lips wide to put him into her mouth.

He gasped, but he didn't tell her to stop.

She sucked him. Bobbed her head up and down. Suctioning. Licking. Getting horny herself as she remembered his slick and hard cock inside her.

She moaned and moved in time to her strokes and then gasped as he manhandled her upward for a kiss. His hands shoved at her track pants—the sexy outfit she'd chosen to wear. Her attitude being: take me as I am.

He did.

In the car, on the side of the road, with vehicles zipping fast.

She didn't care.

But the cop did.

15

Embarrassment had Anika ducked in her seat the rest of the way into town, whereas Dominick wore a wide grin.

Yeah, he'd gotten a warning for fucking his girlfriend in public. As if he could have done anything less when she decided to blow him.

She was so goddamned perfect it hurt.

As they reached the pet store, she composed herself enough to say, "I don't usually do that kind of thing."

"That's because you and me, we're special."

"And now criminals."

"Indecent exposure is just a misdemeanor. Don't worry. It won't go on your permanent record." He winked playfully.

Him.

Playful.

She brought out the softer, more fun side of him.

"What kind of catnip are we buying?" she asked as they headed for the entrance.

"Dunno. Depends what they got. Maybe one of everything?"

"You know it sounds nuts, right?"

"I do." They headed for the store, and the moment they entered, his chin lifted, and he sniffed. "Can you smell that?" Faint yet delicious.

"If you mean wet dog…" She grimaced over at the washing station where canines were getting a bath.

"I'm talking about something sweet. Follow me." Because his nose had chosen a direction. They threaded the aisles to the one labelled, *Feline Treats*. As they entered the aisle, he scanned the shelves and read labels. Dried meat. Weird processed crap. A section on catnip that had him licking his lips, but the things that drew his eye were the trays of fluffy green grass.

He rubbed his hand over it. Soft. Nice. If he had a big enough patch, he'd love to roll naked on it. However, at seven ninety-seven each, it would cost him well over a hundred bucks to buy enough of them.

But they weren't the source of the smell he

sought. Anika found it. "Hey, Dom. Check this out. They actually sell catnip plants."

He reached for the potted plants and lifted them to his face. He stuck his nose against it for a deep whiff. He then bit off a leaf and ate it. It tasted so fucking amazing.

"Dom, what are you doing?" she hissed.

"I can't help myself. It's sooooo good." The words emerged on a low growl. For a second, it worried him. A man did not growl in public. He saved it for the bedroom when pleasuring his lady.

He held the plant away from his mouth. It didn't look appetizing. Yet, every time he took a breath, he wanted more.

Maybe just one more bite.

Anika wouldn't let him. She tugged at the pot. "You can't just start chomping on the plant in the store."

She didn't understand. It was delicious. He didn't just want another bite. He needed it.

Needed.

He retook possession of his plant.

Chomp.

"Dom! No!"

Once more, she tried to steal it.

Mine. He held it firmly and growled. It shocked him enough that he managed to push down the pressure inside him trying to burst free.

He had to keep control.

Needed to not scare Anika.

Might be too late. Her wide eyes showed that she was pretty freaked out.

A guy approached, reed-thin, with a hooked nose. "Sir, I have to ask that you not eat the plant." He dared to hold out his hand.

Dom snarled, and the clerk recoiled. Pussy. He could eat him if he wanted.

"Sir. You need to leave the store."

He would but only because he wanted to take his plants home. He snared a second pot and, with one in each hand, headed for the exit. Feeling more and more strange.

His clothes chafed.

"Sir, what are you doing? You haven't paid for those. I'm going to call the cops."

He heard his female murmuring behind him. He exited the store and hit the light rain. Lifted his face to it with a grimace.

He hated getting wet. But his plant liked it. The smell deepened. Tempted.

Mmm.

He chewed another leaf and then an entire shoot to the stalk.

His female exited. "What the hell was that about? You're now banned from the store because the guy thinks you're high on something."

I am.

He remained cognizant enough to realize the catnip plant did something to him. Felt good. Amazing. Drowsy. Seriously, though his eyes remained open, it was as if he fell asleep mentally.

"Get me home." Somewhere safe so he could nap.

"You don't look good." Alarm spiked her scent.

He glanced at his arms. Covered in dark fuzz. "Wass happenin'?" The words emerged with a rolling burr.

"Get in the car." She opened the door for him, and he sat in the seat, plants in his lap.

So nice. He petted the leaves. Took another bite when she wasn't looking.

Finished swallowing by the time she sat down beside him.

His body pulsed. Pushed him to close off his consciousness.

He pushed back. He couldn't go to sleep now. Not with his female angry.

"What the fuck is wrong with you?" she hissed as she drove them away.

He managed a slurred, "Canna stop." He really couldn't, even as he knew it was wrong.

"You're behaving really weird," she stated as she drove. "Do you think this is what happened to your brother? Maybe a sensitivity to catnip is a family thing."

"Not related to Tyson," he mumbled, staring at his hands. Noticed the nails elongating. Felt his jaw popping. And he really hated his clothes right now.

"Maybe it's because of the environment where you were raised. Something in the water."

He didn't know what ailed him. He still felt good but itchy. More than itchy.

Confined.

"Stopppp!" he barked.

Even before she'd pulled to the side of the road near a construction site for new housing, he was opening the door and throwing himself out. He hit the ground and dropped the plants. He didn't care that they spilled. He pulled at his shirt. His pants.

Get it off.

Off!

The moment he could stretch, he roared. Then he was running, hands and feet, fleet of foot. Keen of sight.

Ready to hunt.

16

As the panther—that used to be Dom until he went all Transformer—suddenly raced off, Anika blinked.

What. The. Fuck just happened? Surely, she'd not seen a man, naked as the day he was born, suddenly scrabbling on all fours, his body reshaping into something hairy with a tail.

A fucking tail.

Perhaps she dreamed—she pinched herself.

Ouch.

Did it again, just in case.

Definitely awake. She got out of the car and breathed deeply. She had just about calmed down when the panther stalked out from behind the bull-dozer and leapt up onto the shovel.

"Dom?" A tremulous syllable.

The feline head turned her way, and they locked gazes. Her heart stopped.

The panther leapt down and trotted farther into the construction site.

"Dom, come back!" She didn't understand what'd happened. People did not turn into cats. Seeing the plants on the ground, she scowled.

"I blame you," she growled before picking them up. Dominick had acted oddly from the moment he started sniffing them. Not to mention, what possessed him to eat them to begin with?

He obviously reacted to the catnip. Or was she the one drugged? Because, after all, she'd seen a man turn into a cat.

Again. What. The. Fuck?

She glanced at the mostly quiet construction site with its heaps of supplies, a trailer for management, and a few dormant machines. Last she'd heard via the rumor mill, it'd gotten shut down because of COVID-19. After all the mandatory closures, it had tried to stay afloat, and then the heavily conditioned reopening rules happened. Some places could survive the restrictions, but some found it easier to fold. It didn't help that each time someone tested positive or came into contact with someone positive, the contract tracing closed them down. It made for angry clients. The company ended up throwing in the towel.

It happened all too often. Pity, because she'd heard they were supposed to build an apartment building geared toward those with lower incomes.

The closure meant high metal struts set up and waiting for concrete to be poured.

Dom—the cat—could be anywhere. And, honestly, she was kind of scared to find him. It. What the fuck?

She took a few steps and stooped to grab his clothes, the shirt torn in his desperation to remove it.

The shoes exploded as the paws and claws had torn through them.

Paws.

She sat on her haunches and hung her head, breathing hard. This had to be a dream. This kind of thing didn't happen.

I saw it with my own eyes.

I'm not crazy.

Dominick was out there somewhere. Possibly scared. Maybe she could coax him back into being a man?

She took a few steps into the construction yard. "Dom? Are you there? Can you hear me?"

No reply, but she felt watched. She glanced around at the various spots he could hide. Him... something else.

She shivered. Maybe it wasn't a good idea to

confront a panther alone. Problem being, how was she to get help while not coming across as crazy when she explained what she'd seen?

She placed his clothes in the car along with the surviving plant. She still didn't get it. She found the aroma off-putting. It made Dom's behavior that much odder.

If it doesn't affect me, then maybe there really is something in the water at his house. Two genetically unrelated people, reacting oddly to the same non-psychotropic substance?

His family needed to know. It was the right thing to do, even as she grimaced on the way there.

She practiced what she'd say to his mom. "So, hey, Dom had an incident with catnip. He is now a panther."

Not *thought* he was a giant cat, actually fucking *was* a massive pussy.

She parked in the driveway and groaned. No one would ever believe her.

Someone needed to know, though.

Getting out of the car, with the plant in hand, she knocked on the front door of the house. No one answered.

She banged again, only now realizing that she was the only car. She bit her lip. "Fuck." Now what?

A staticky sound preceded a brusque, "Dom's not here."

Raymond! The reclusive brother in the basement.

She couldn't see whatever camera he used and hoped it had sound. "I know Dom's not. He was with me. But... Um... Something happened. He needs help."

"Come inside. I'm in the basement." *Bzzt.* The door unlocked.

She entered and made three wrong guesses before finding a door with stairs going down. The wooden steps appeared archaic, yet the setup once she reached the floor was anything but.

The walls and even the ceiling appeared covered in padding, dimpled where it was pinned in place. The floor bore a smooth laminate. On one side of the basement lurked a furnace, hot water tank, and the electrical box. Under the stairs, boxes labelled *Xmas*. Against one wall, about a dozen bearing the letter *D*.

Which left two more walls, lined with screens, each displaying something different. Under them, a series of desks pushed to run along the wall, littered with an assortment of shit. Beakers. Electronics. Test tubes, and what looked like a fridge and a strange metal oven.

There was a cot in the room, and a gaming chair on wheels. Nothing else for comfort.

Sitting on the moving seat, Raymond spun to eye her.

"Where's my brother? What's wrong with him?"

She held out the catnip pot that'd survived, and Raymond's nose twitched. "What is that?"

"Catnip. Dom started eating it in the store and got a little crazy."

"Was he arrested?"

She shook her head. "Actually, it's weirder than that."

"Let me guess, he turned into a wild animal."

17

Raymond knew.

How did he know?

"What the fuck is going on?" she exclaimed.

"It's what I've been trying to figure out. It all started with me thinking my drones were hacked. Because who turns from a boy into a cat? Not my little brother Tyson. Problem is, no one broke into my machines. Which means, the video had to be real."

"What video? You'll need to explain better because you're not making any sense."

Raymond spun from her and began typing. "The drone footage I got last night. It's easier to show you." A video feed appeared, perspective from above, showing a grainy image done in hues of green. A night vision camera that showed a human shape turning into something four-legged with a tail.

"That's your little brother?"

"I know it's hard to tell. I really need to upgrade my camera, but I've been investing in other stuff," he grumbled. He changed the video feeds on screen to what appeared to be lab results.

"What is that?" She pointed.

"Something Stefan suggested when I showed the video to him this morning. Bloodwork results for our family. Stefan had them done, all of us except for Daeve, Maeve's twin, and his other sister, Jessie. They've been busy the last little while."

"And? What does this have to do with that footage?"

"Just that, despite not being bound by blood, every single Hubbard kid has a similar mutation."

"What are you talking about? What kind of mutation?"

"I don't know yet. I won't make any hypotheses without further study, other than to predict that catnip is a trigger for it in both Tyson's and Dominick's cases."

She glanced at the plant in her hand. "No shit." Catnip was Dominick's spinach. The inanest comparison to come to mind. Still, both were green. Although, in Popeye's case, he got stronger and saved Olive.

In hers, Dom went furry and ran away.

Dear God.

She'd slept with him. Bestiality was a crime. Only he was a man when it'd happened.

And he'd not worn a condom the last times. She couldn't help but panic, even though she was on the pill.

"I'm just surprised he's susceptible," he mused aloud. "After all, this isn't the first time he'd have been exposed."

"Unless you own a cat or hang out with someone who does, not really. I mean, I know of catnip, and this is the first time I've ever seen the plant." She waggled it.

Raymond swallowed. "Would you mind putting that thing across the room? It's distracting."

"Hold on, you're allergic to it, too?" An adverse reaction. That had to be it.

"Told you, we all share the same genetic twist. Kind of. We each have slight variations to it."

"You're not making any sense."

"Because it *doesn't* make sense." Raymond raked a hand through his hair, making it stand on end.

"Listen, I don't know what's wrong with your family. What I do know is Dominick turned into a panther and ran off." There, she'd said it aloud.

Raymond didn't mock her. "Where?"

"Some construction site in town. I left because I didn't know what to do."

Ray grimaced. "Me, either. I assume he didn't bring his phone with him?"

She shook her head. "I've got his stuff in the car. He kind of half-stripped, half-exploded out of his clothes when he changed."

"Damn." Raymond rubbed his chin. "That makes finding him complicated."

"And what will we do when we find him? How do we change him back?"

"I don't know." It was the most chilling answer of all.

"How do we find him?"

"We need to go back to where he took off on you."

"Now?" A stupid reply, and yet her alarm went off, a reminder set on her phone in case she got distracted so she wasn't late for work.

How could she go to work when Dom was lost? Still, she couldn't afford to lose a day's pay.

Sounded callous to even think it, and yet, she had bills that wouldn't take a break. And, realistically, what could she do? Dom had turned into a panther. Didn't they tend to maul people?

Her mind flashed to Thomas. Attacked by a wild cat, he'd said.

Oh, fuck.

EVE LANGLAIS

Should she tell Raymond? It might make a difference. "I think he's done this before. Turned into a panther."

"When? What makes you think that?"

"My ex got attacked last night by what he claims was a wild panther."

Raymond's mouth rounded. "Shit. That's not good. What if he goes after someone else? Animal control would be called. He'd get shot."

"We have to find him." *We* because she had to help.

"Let's start with that construction zone."

It didn't take long to drive there.

Raymond got out of her car and frowned at the machinery and the barren ground. "I doubt he'd have stayed here long. Shitty hunting and too exposed. Add in the fact I'm not getting pinged about any reports of a cat on any emergency channels, and it seems safe to say he's moved on."

"How are we supposed to know where he went?" She glanced around. Where to start?

"If he's a cat, is he moving by instinct, or is he still cognizant inside?"

She remembered what he'd said about his blackouts. "I don't think he knows what's happening."

"So, instinct then." Raymond glanced around and frowned. "What does an animal do if dropped into unfamiliar territory?"

"He heads for home." The answer slipped from her lips.

"Maybe. But if he doesn't, then it makes sense for us to split up. I'll see if I can find his trail on this end, and you go to the house and wait."

"Leave you here? How will you get back?"

"I've already texted Stefan to help."

"Oh." It occurred to her how many people would know the crazy secret she'd imparted. What if she were mistaken? "Won't your family find it weird if they see me parked at your house?"

"Mom's gonna be gone for at least another hour or so. Maybe we can find him before she knows something's wrong. Maeve already left for work. Given she just got that job, I won't bug her quite yet. Plus, your laundry is still there. It gives you the perfect excuse. I tossed it into the dryer, by the way."

"Thank you. Sorry. Dom kind of insisted we go to the pet store."

"It's fine. If you're with my brother, then that makes you a new sister."

She wanted to say they weren't together, only to realize the idea sat very well with her. She wouldn't mind trying it out for a bit.

"What do I do if he comes back?"

"Depends on what shape he's in. If he's a naked man, toss him a blanket."

149

"And if he's not?" If he remained a jungle cat with big teeth and claws?

"Open a can of tuna."

Not the most reassuring advice. Still, at least she had a plan. She drove back to the farm and sat in her parked car for a minute.

This was crazy.

She should leave now. Run away from the guy who transformed when around catnip.

But then she remembered the man. Who swaggered to her defense. Who said the stupidest things, and yet could be the sweetest when he talked about how he felt about her.

Then she thought of the fact that, if the roles were reversed, he'd most definitely be looking for her.

She eyed the forest by his place. Did she dare go into the trees?

No, but she could sit by the edge and call for him.

Sitting with her legs lotus-style, she put her hands on her knees and closed her eyes, took some deep, cleansing breaths. A calming exercise she'd learned in therapy, usually to deal with her Thomas anxiety, but it worked on other kinds, as well.

She heard nothing but the gentle sloughing of the wind through the branches. She couldn't have said how long she waited. She'd heard a motorcycle at one point—someone arriving at the farmhouse. But she didn't turn.

Didn't want to deal with someone mocking what she'd told Raymond. It was hard to believe that it'd even happened. It was such a gorgeous autumn day. The sun shone. The bugs still hummed here and there—not as copious as in spring. The leaves on the trees hadn't yet started to fall but had begun their shift from green to red and yellow.

As she breathed and dropped into a Zen moment, all the distractions around her disappeared. Literally, all noise stopped. She'd not realized how many were in the background until they went silent.

I'm not alone.

"Dominick? Are you out there?" she whispered. No way would he have heard her. No way was it him. The distance from the house to the site was too far. He couldn't have walked here this fast. Unless he ran on four fleet feet.

Crack. Her mouth went dry. She wasn't alone.

She couldn't help but open her eyes and watch. Stare while holding her breath as a massive black cat stalked from the tree line, head low. It slunk, gazing at her with eyes she recognized. Too human in the face of an animal.

"Dom?" She hated the tremor in the single syllable.

It crept closer, and her heart raced even as she forgot to breathe.

Oh my God. I'm going to die. Eaten by her kitty-transformer boyfriend.

Instead of pouncing and eating her face, the panther got close enough to lie down and place his head in her lap.

It seemed only natural to drag her fingers through his fur, each stroke easing the tension in her. Releasing muscles gone rigid. Until her heart rate and breathing returned to normal, only to suddenly tense when the big kitty purred.

Panthers couldn't purr. Then again, humans couldn't change into animals, either.

Her phone buzzed, but she couldn't check the message. She was too afraid to move.

She worried that someone in Dom's family would startle him. But they remained alone.

And she saw—felt...experienced—when fur turned to flesh. Panther into man.

The thing that finally sent her sanity over the edge.

18

Dominick felt good. Head in the lap of his girlfriend. He could smell her. If he turned his face, he could taste her.

Yet, instead of sighing in pleasure when he tried, she squeaked and dumped him out of her lap.

He rolled to his back and blinked. "What the fuck?"

"You tell me. What the fuck is going on? Why didn't you tell me you could turn into a panther?"

"What?" The contentment and languorous feeling left quickly as he confronted Anika's frightened mien. "I don't understand. How did I get here? What happened?"

She bit her lower lip. "What's the last thing you remember?"

"The pet store. And some twerp telling me I

should leave." Then…nothing. Oh, fuck. He'd blacked out. Given his naked gangly bits plus Anika's fright, he'd done something bad.

"You don't remember telling me to stop the car? Getting out and stripping?" She swallowed and looked down before softly adding, "I saw you turn into a big black cat."

"That's impossible." He rubbed his face.

"I saw it!" she hotly exclaimed.

"It can't be."

"Then explain it."

"I had a blackout and scared you, obviously. But no matter how weird I was acting, I assure you, I am a hundred percent man." So long as he ignored his dreams.

"No. You weren't." Flatly said, and it chilled him. Because he did remember some stuff that made no sense on the surface. Unless she spoke the truth.

He glanced down. "No fur now at any rate."

"It's the catnip. It does something to you. Makes you into a beast."

The words chilled him because they reminded him of what the police had said happened to Thomas. A wild animal attack on a night where he could remember nothing after chugging the catnip juice.

It couldn't be true.

"I think I need a drink." He got to his feet and

felt the autumn air on his bare cheeks and, worse, sucking the heat from his shrinking ball sac. A good thing she'd met his cock on a good day, because right now, he wouldn't impress anyone.

She kept a socially distanced space between them as she accompanied him. "I should text your brother to let him know we're on our way."

"I'd rather not tell him about my incident."

"Too late."

He paused mid-step. "Stefan knows?"

"I assume so by now. Would Raymond have told him?"

He groaned. "Ray, too?"

It was worse than that. Mom and Tyson waited on the front porch.

The moment Dominick's mom saw him, her eyes widened, and she whipped off her apron and had Tyson run it over.

Because wearing her Hug-the-Cook apron was so much better.

As Dominick neared, he noticed his mom biting her lip. Worried. So very worried.

"Are you okay?" she asked.

He tried to make light of the situation. "Apparently, little brother here isn't the only one who thinks he's a cat when a certain herb is around."

"Thinks?" Stefan drawled, grinding out his cigarette and approaching. "When is this family going to have a sit-down chat about the fact we're not quite human?"

"Don't be ridiculous...." Dominick trailed off as he saw his mother's face.

The terror and resignation.

"Oh, fuck. Mom. Do you know something?"

She glanced at Anika and kept her lips pressed.

"This is my cue to go." Anika headed for her car, even as he blurted out, "No."

He followed her, but she whirled and shook her head. "I can't stay. This is all..." She stopped talking and eyed her feet before she sighed. "I like you, Dom. A lot. But this is too much for me. Too strange. I don't know what to think or feel. I need time to process this."

"And you think I don't?"

"I'm sure you're even more messed up than I am right now. Which is why I should go. Talk with your mom and family. Figure out what's going on."

"What about us?" Because, right now, that concerned him more.

She pressed her lips into a thin line. "We'll talk later."

"Promise?" A part of him didn't want to let her leave. Wanted to throw her over his shoulder and drag her into the house. But at the same time, he could understand her confusion.

Hell, he was reeling and struggling with what

she'd told him. Anika wouldn't lie, and yet, how could he be a shapeshifter? A panther? A killer. Thomas had survived, but he could have just as easily taken the man's life. Perhaps it was best she left before he hurt her, too.

He dragged her close for a kiss. She clung to him, her mouth hot against his. At least she didn't recoil from his touch. It gave him hope, even as his heart sank as he watched her taillights going up the road.

Only then did he pivot and glare at his mom. "Do you have something you want to tell me?"

She looked small in that moment as she said, "I was hoping I'd never have to tell any of you."

"Tell us what?"

"My brother made you in a lab."

19

MOM

Nana Hubbard had truly hoped this day would never come. It wasn't because she wanted to lie to her children. More like it remained the best way to protect them.

"What do you mean your brother made us in a lab?" Dominick yelled.

"I… Uh…" For once, she was without words.

Stefan, though, had a few. "Give her a break."

"No!"

"Calm down," his brother cajoled.

"Fuck being calm. I'm a fucking freak." Her oldest struggled with his emotions. With reason.

"Mom's not the enemy." Stefan did his best to protect her even as she deserved Dominick's anger.

"She lied," growled her hurting boy.

"Yeah, and she's gonna explain herself. Right mom?"

"I'll tell you everything," she agreed even as she'd prayed this day would never come.

"I gotta fetch Raymond. He's in town pounding pavement, looking for your dumb ass. Pretty sure he'll want to hear this."

"My dumb ass?" Dominick growled. "How was I supposed to know I'd turn into a fucking beast if I ate catnip?"

"That's my fault. Guess I should have warned you," Stefan declared as he held out his hand to Mom. "Can I borrow the van? Because I doubt Ray's gonna want to ride bitch with me."

Nana tossed him her keys, which jangled as Stefan caught them.

"I don't want to wait," Dominick grumbled.

"Too fucking bad," Stefan snapped. "You will wait. Have a can of tuna. Shit is delicious, trust me, I know."

"Not hungry," was the sullen reply.

"Then play with some string. Fuck, lick your balls or hunt some mice. I don't fucking care what you do, but make sure it involves showering and some clothes. No one wants to see your junk."

"Asshole." Huffed as he headed upstairs.

Stefan pressed his lips together but didn't say a word as he left.

With feet gone wooden, Nana headed to the kitchen, the one place she felt comfortable. She made a big pot of coffee with a little something-something in it. She needed the extra help.

Sitting down, she was soon joined by a rarely silent Tyson. He'd had a stressful day of doctor's tests as she'd come to grips with what his episode with the catnip meant.

What am I going to do, Johan?

Her brother was dead and couldn't help her. She was alone for the first time in a long while, even as many of her children surrounded her. Curious expressions adorned some of their faces—Pammy and Tyson. Anger on others—Maeve and Dominick. Pity on Stefan's.

What did he know? How long had he known it?

Daphne had been allowed to go to a playdate after school. She was too young to understand. Heck, even Tyson might find it hard to handle. However, after what'd happened to him, she had no choice.

Time for the truth to come out.

Maeve broke the silence. "What the fuck is going on?"

"Language," Nana said, more out of practice than care.

"Fuck language, Mom." Dominick bristled. "What the fuck is going on? What's wrong with me and Tyson? What do you mean, your brother *made* us?"

"Slow down a second and let me catch up," Pammy interrupted, unimpressed she'd been asked to leave work early for a family meeting. It was only the fact that none had ever been called before that convinced her to make the trip to Richmond from Gloucester. "You're telling me that Dommy and Ty got high on catnip and turned into cats?"

"I can show you what we have so far as proof, if it helps."

Ray played the video footage from the drone, showing Tyson's transformation—not the most convincing evidence. They all became true believers upon seeing the panther emerge from the woods and lay in Anika's lap. And then he was a man.

"Well, fuck me to hell and back," Pammy huffed.

"Language!" Tyson squeaked.

It almost made Nana smile, but fear kept her serious. Especially because, once the videos were done, they wanted answers.

"What the fuck is going on, Mom?" Dommy asked, gentler than before.

"So it was catnip for you, too?" Nana asked, wanting to be sure. "Odd, because you were highly allergic to it when you were young."

"Did I turn into a kitty cat then, too?" he snapped.

"No. The fact you couldn't is the reason you were deemed unsuitable," she supplied softly.

That snapped his mouth shut.

"You knew he could turn into a panther."

"Actually, what I knew was that he couldn't. Which is how he—and all of you—ended up in my care." He'd been her first orphan.

"You knew we were different."

"That's just it. I got you only because you weren't. You were created to be something more than human. And when it failed... It got complicated." She rubbed her forehead.

"I don't care how fucking messy it is. We have a right to know." The children let Dominick, the oldest, make the demand.

"Even if knowing could be dangerous?"

"I'd say not knowing has proven more hazardous," Stefan offered. He dangled an unlit cigarette from his lips.

"Have you morphed, too?" Nana asked.

"Don't change the subject."

"You don't understand. If you're changing, then you're in danger. If anyone realizes what you are, where you came from..." Her throat tightened as she said, "I don't know if I can keep you safe."

"Fuck me. We're hiding from the government!" Raymond exclaimed. "No wonder I couldn't find a goddamned trace of us in any system."

"You were looking?" Nana shouldn't have been so shocked. Raymond always had an insatiable curiosity.

"I was adopted. No offense, Mom, I love you, but I wanted to know where I came from. When I couldn't find anything, I looked into the whole family. We don't exist. And you never had a brother."

She bit her lip. "I did, but he was wiped out by the company he worked for."

She'd not noticed Stefan slipping away. He was leaning on the doorjamb one minute, gone the next. But she noticed his return because a few heads turned at his approach. Tyson, Dominick, Raymond. Maeve grimaced and said, "Ew. What is that awful smell?"

"Catnip," Nana announced. "And keep it away from your sister. From the sounds of it, she might still be allergic."

"That smells so good." Tyson lunged for the plant, but before he could snare it, Dominick grabbed the pot.

He hugged it. "Mine."

Tyson hissed.

Eyes wide, Maeve watched them both and exclaimed, "What has gotten into you both?"

It seemed obvious to Nana, but today's youth didn't have the same critical-thinking skills as in her day. "The catnip is making them high."

"What?" Maeve blinked. "But they're not cats."

"You saw the video," Nana pointed out.

"Which I still think has to be a trick. I swear, if I'm being pranked, I will lose my shit."

"It's not a joke, Maeve." Nana only wished it were because she feared what the truth would do to her family.

Dominick held the grass out of reach of his brother. Barely. Tyson was only a few inches shorter.

Stefan had a reach better than both of them. He snared the pot, opened the back door, and tossed it.

The tension in the room eased. Tyson flushed and sat down.

Dominick did, too.

"So, let's hear the story of our creation and why it involves catnip for some of us." Stefan remained casual, yet Nana knew her boy. Knew he understood more of what was going on than the rest did.

"Are you affected by catnip, or is it something else?"

Stefan offered a tight smile. "I've learned to control it. By myself I might add, since I assumed for a long time that I was the only freak in the family."

"You, too?" Dominick sputtered.

Tyson, on the other hand, relaxed. "Thank fuck it's not just me."

"Language!" This time, it was Maeve barking it.

"What are you all talking about? I don't understand."

"Does anyone need cookies? I could whip some up. They'll be ready in twelve minutes." She needed to do something with her hands.

"No." Synchronized and firm. Nana slumped.

To her surprise, Stefan was the one to come by her side and put an arm around her. "No matter what you did, one thing is clear. You loved us. And we love you. That won't change."

"Unless you made us freaks," Dominick clarified.

"You're not freaks," she hotly rebutted.

"Notice she didn't deny having a hand in our making?" Tyson was the one to sound bitter.

"I didn't, but I knew the person who did, and I did nothing to stop it. Couldn't. Because if I had, we'd all be dead."

Maeve stood. "I'm making cookies."

"I'll—"

Her daughter glared her down. "You will sit and speak loudly as you start explaining."

The secret she'd held for so long was about to come out.

She took a deep breath and began her tale. "Thirty years ago, I was visiting my brother, Johan. He worked for some super-secret research lab. So secret I wasn't allowed to know its name or location. Not that I cared. I was just in Edmonton to visit him

EVE LANGLAIS

and go sightseeing. I'd just gotten divorced, you see." She'd felt adrift. In her late thirties, childless, and starting over.

"Blah. Blah. Get to the point." Maeve snapped, hands deep in dough.

"I'm trying. It began over lunch." In an Italian restaurant, because Johan knew how she loved her pasta.

They'd barely sat down, and she saw him fidgeting. Obviously upset.

"What's wrong?"

"Nothing."

"You said the same thing when Mary-Anne died." Johan's wife, who'd gotten ovarian cancer. He'd dealt with it on his own. Took stoicism to the extreme. He appeared to be doing the same now. "I can tell something is bugging you. Is it your love life? Are you dying? Need money?"

He shook his head and finally said on a huge sigh, "Believe it or not, I am struggling with morality. I've done lots of bad things in my life. Things I would take back if I could, but none like the choice I'm being given now. I have to do something wrong. Bad. Evil." His chin dropped until it almost hit the table.

"No, you don't. You just said you had a choice."

"It's not that easy." He sounded so morose.

"Is this about your job?"

It took him a moment before he nodded.

"What's your boss want you to do that's so bad?"

166

He didn't spill at first. He pressed his lips together and shook his head. "It's too dangerous."

"Johan." She murmured his name. "You can tell me."

"I can't. I've signed a non-disclosure agreement."

Nana snorted. "You know I won't tell anyone else, and it's obviously bothering you."

"It's more than just the NDA. This entire project I'm doing... It's wrong. I've suspected it for years, and now that I'm working at the very heart of it, it's been confirmed."

"Walk away."

"I can't. He'll kill me."

She blinked at his statement. Johan didn't appear to be jesting. Still... "You're exaggerating. It can't be that bad."

"Oh, but it is. I've been doing evil things, Nanette. Things I'm going to Hell for. But what I've been asked to do now? I can't. I just can't." His head drooped.

She put a hand on his shoulder and leaned close. "Can't do what, Johan?"

His expression remained bleak as he lifted his head to say, "I can't kill a child. It's not his fault he didn't manifest, that he's one hundred percent normal."

She reeled. "Kill a child? What have you gotten involved in?"

"Something bigger than me and you."

"Then tell the authorities."

"I can't," he exclaimed. "Or I'll end up like the previous doctor if anyone ever finds out I told you."

"How am I supposed to avenge you if I don't know what's going on?" was her weak reply.

"No one would believe you if you told them. I still struggle with it myself." Then, as if he'd made a decision, it emerged in a rush. "I'm working on the creation of huanimorphs."

"A what?"

"Huanimorph. The term coined for those who can morph from human to animal."

"Why would anyone want to do that?"

"Ask those in the hundreds of werewolf movies and books. Humans have always wanted to be more. Stronger. Faster. Taking the best of humanity and mixing it with the physical traits of another."

"That's gross."

"It's already happening. Werewolves are real. And not just real; the government knows about them. Even uses them as elite soldiers. But being the military, they want more. And not just wolves. They want soldiers that can swim great distances undetected or that can climb or move stealthily through jungles."

"You're making monsters for the government."

"Not very well," he admitted. "While we've had some successes with the Ursine genome, reptile, and even in tweaking the wolf to create better huanimorphs, we've failed to trigger the same shifting gene in those twisted with feline and avian DNA."

It struck her then. "You're experimenting on children."

She gaped at him. "Is that what you meant by killing a kid?"

"The splicing occurs before gestation, during the embryonic stage."

"I'm confused. Who are you going to kill, then?"

"DK04. He is the only one of the panther litter that survived. He's also just over four years old and still hasn't manifested."

"So, he can't shift into a—a—?"

"Panther."

She blinked. "So what if he can't?"

"He's a failure, and I've been told to terminate."

She gaped at her brother. "You can't kill a child."

"I know." His shoulders sagged. "What else can I do, though? If he doesn't disappear, by my hand, then I will."

She could see that he truly feared for his life. Felt he had no other option. But a recent divorcee with a bit of money to buy a place and settle down did.

"Give him to me."

"What?" Johan's turn to blink at her.

"I said, give me the child. I'll raise him."

"That might not be a good idea. We don't know what will happen as he gets older. He could become dangerous."

"He's a kid in need of a protector." A mother. And she had a chance to make a family.

That night, under the guise of darkness, DK04, who would become Dominick, was smuggled out, and Nana drove across several provinces before settling in Ontario. She started out in Sudbury, but the long winters sent her fleeing within a few years, along with a second son and a daughter. They moved to Ottawa, where she bought a farm and continued receiving kids until Johan died.

There was silence in the kitchen as she finished.

Nana glanced at Dominick. "I'm sorry I lied to you. To all of you. In my defense, I just wanted to give you the home and love you deserved."

"You saved me. You saved all of us," Stefan murmured.

Whereas Raymond was on his laptop. "Says your brother died in a car crash."

She nodded. "He was about to retire and feared for his life. But he didn't want to leave until he managed to get one last child out."

"Daphne?"

She shook her head. "He died the night he was supposed to meet me. I never got the kid."

"Does the secret lab he worked for know he smuggled us out to you?"

She shrugged. "I always assumed no since they didn't show up on our front step. I changed your names. Even mine isn't the same anymore. I kept my married one. I stopped visiting him publicly, but we kept in touch via secure chat systems. Every few years, he'd ask me if I could take another one. How could I say no?"

"Your brother would have killed us if you'd not

rescued us," Maeve pointed out, slamming the oven door shut. "And you didn't stop him."

"He would have died if I'd told anyone. And I feared what would happen to you," Nana explained. It sounded weak, but Dominick agreed.

"Mom did the right thing."

Tyson added, "We've all seen the *X-men*. I don't know about you, but I ain't letting no one lock my ass up to use me as a guinea pig for testing."

"So, are we all panthers, then?" Maeve asked.

"No. You're each different."

"I'm a tiger," Stefan offered, which actually made sense with his ginger locks.

Tyson sounded sheepish when he admitted, "When I was high, I thought I was a lion."

Nana nodded. "That's correct. Raymond is a lynx, and Maeve, you and your brother are bears."

"That explains a lot," muttered Tyson.

"Watch your mouth, or I'll bite off your tail," Maeve growled.

"What about me?" Pammy asked.

"You're a tiger-mix like Stefan. Jessie got wolf, and Daphne is our falcon."

"She can fly?" Tyson exclaimed.

"Not that I know of. The avian huanimorphs never succeeded, as far as I know."

"This is insane." Dominick rubbed his face. "This

morning, I was just a nice, normal guy, waking up with his girlfriend."

"Since when do you have a girlfriend?" Tyson asked.

"Since he ran into his high school flame. It's true love," Maeve drawled.

It was, and Nana loved the blush on his cheeks. She just wished she didn't have to offer the following warning. Had hoped she'd never have to say anything.

"Now might be a good time to mention that with a few of you manifesting, there have been issues with the whole baby-making aspect." According to her brother, humans couldn't handle a huanimorph fetus. The mothers miscarried them early on. As for the huanimorphs themselves? The females appeared infertile.

The news sent Maeve fleeing.

But her boys…they had a lot more questions. She cooked while she answered them.

Didn't need any salt, though; her tears did the trick.

20

Anika meant to go home after leaving Dominick. She also thought about turning around and going back because, dammit, she wanted answers, too.

But as she neared town and saw the sign for her work, she decided she didn't want to be alone. Despite having texted Darryl that she might not make it in, she parked and threw on the clothes she kept in her back seat. Might as well work. The dull drone of it would help clear her thoughts. Maybe.

How was she supposed to reconcile what'd happened? Her boyfriend was a jungle cat.

How did that happen? Why?

On her break, she conducted searches on people who could change into animals. She mostly got stuff about werewolves, but Native Americans used to speak of them, as well. In their legends, they became many different animals.

But the one common themes among them was that it could be contagious, and they were dangerous.

However, even she had to admit Dominick was the gentlest of pussycats compared to Thomas, who waited by her car as she exited the store—sent home a half-hour early because she told Darryl she wasn't feeling well. When he dared question, she asked him if he had any spare underpants and tampons she could borrow.

Darryl couldn't let her punch out quickly enough. She'd hurried to her car, having decided to call Dominick and talk things out. Seeing Thomas with his angry brows slowed her steps.

Not him again.

"Shouldn't you be recovering from your alley cat encounter?" She mocked him despite knowing the truth.

"You think you're so fucking funny. Sending that *thing* after me. Joke's on you. The cops might not believe me, but she does."

"Who?" As if it were a signal, a door opened on the car Anika had just passed.

She whirled. Too late. Her arm was caught before she could properly struggle, and then both of her hands were snared in front of her.

"What the fuck?" was her exclamation, the reply being her ass getting shoved into the passenger seat of a car.

What the hell just happened?

Thomas smirked as he neared. "That was nicely done. Now, she can't fight me."

"Don't you lay a hand on her." A woman's voice. The same one who'd just captured Anika. Sleek dark brown hair, cut in layers a few inches past her shoulders. Slim-figured and looking at Thomas with a don't-give-a-fuck stare.

Thomas didn't like her command. "I'll do whatever I like to my ex-whore."

"You really are a piece of shit." The woman grabbed him by the back of the head and slammed it off her knee.

Thomas dropped, and she stepped over him to slam the car door shut.

Oh, shit.

The woman got in on the other side, and Anika pressed as far away from her as possible.

"Who are you? What do you want with me?"

Eyes of the most amazing hazel-gold peered at her. "I'm not actually after you. But I do have questions about your boyfriend."

"I don't have a boyfriend," was her faint reply.

"Are you sure? Because your ex-husband says you

do. A big dude who turns into an even bigger cat. Sound familiar?"

"No." Whispered through dry lips.

"Are you lying or just ignorant? Guess we'll soon find out. Text him."

"Who?"

"Who do you think? Tell your boyfriend you've been kidnapped and he's to come to the cemetery by the church. Alone. If he doesn't, bad things will happen to you."

Because her day hadn't been shit already...

21

AROUND EIGHT THIRTY, DOMINICK AND Stefan ended up outside. His brother to have a smoke, Dominick to grip the rail and try to contain his anger that warred with relief. He finally had a reason for his blackouts and the pressure he felt.

He had something inside him. An animal. Another entity that wanted out.

Which led to anger that his mother had lied.

Hurt, too. Along with disappointment that Stefan had known but hadn't told him. Then again, without proof, would Dominick have believed? He still had a hard time wrapping his head around it, and he'd seen the video of himself emerging from the woods, changing in Anika's lap.

No wonder she'd run away the first chance she got.

"What do you think of the story?" he asked his brother, who blew smoke rings.

"I don't think Mom is lying. I believe it's exactly as she said it happened. With one difference. I have a hard time believing they didn't know."

"What?" Dominick gave his brother a startled glance.

"Come on. Surely, a company as secretive as the one our uncle worked for would have noticed this uncle of ours smuggling something kid-sized out of there. Add in the fact that a bunch of kids suddenly appeared in his sister's life around the same time they rid themselves of failures, and..."

Dominick winced. "Ouch."

"Truth. They tossed us out like garbage because they thought we weren't good enough to be in their monstermorph club."

"Guess they were wrong," was his wry reply. "How long have you known about the catnip thing?"

"First time it happened was in high school at a sleepover. Cat dropped a catnip toy on me. Next thing I knew, I was tearing it open, eating it, and acting crazy." Stefan shrugged. "I was addicted to the stuff for a few years. Used to wake up in the weirdest fucking places. Always naked. You should see my juvenile arrest sheet. All of them had indecent exposure."

Dominick blinked at him. "How did I not know?"

"You enlisted at eighteen. Mom thought I was on drugs and grounded me. I cleaned up and graduated with honors. That fall, I moved into a dorm at university. One with a park and a zoo I could use to safely explore what happened to me when I took catnip. Imagine my surprise when I realized that I didn't just think I was a tiger when high, I actually turned into one."

"Hold on, are you saying you hung out with the tigers at the zoo?"

"I was exploring my other side. Thought maybe I could communicate."

"And?"

Stefan rolled his shoulders. "They aren't crazy about outsiders."

"You said you were addicted to the catnip. But I saw you with the plant. You didn't go nuts like me and Tyson."

"Because I learned control. Which wasn't easy. I've always been more into the vices than you. However, you can't let addiction control you."

Dominick pinched the spot between his eyes. "I don't know if I can help myself. Even smelling it makes me go a little nuts."

"Give it time. You're still new to it."

Dominick snorted. "Time. Do you think that will help Anika not think of me as a freak?"

"She appeared a tad upset when she left."

"She hates me," was his morose reply.

"More like she experienced a great shock. Once she realizes you're still the same annoying dumbfuck as before, she'll get over it."

"You think?" he asked, not sure why Stefan's appraisal meant so much.

"She will, but don't let her stew too long about it. Go see her. Talk to her. Maybe mention keeping it a secret. If I'm right, and the lab that made us is keeping tabs, then we can't have them finding out their experiment worked."

"Guess I'd better ask Mom to borrow the keys to the van." He grimaced. The damn thing was epically emasculating.

Stefan took pity. "Take my bike."

"How you gonna get home?" Stefan wasn't one for public transit.

"I think I'll spend the night. After all, it is Thanksgiving tomorrow."

Dominick grinned. "And that means blueberry waffles for breakfast."

"With whipped cream."

They both drooled for a second before finding their respective balls. "I'll be back by tomorrow with it."

"Just three rules. No crashing. No sex on my seat. And fill up the tank with the premium shit or die."

Dominick left his brother and welcomed the

throb of the bike, the growl of its engine, and the speed that helped clear his mind. He was heading to Anika's apartment when it occurred to him that she might still be at work. He whipped around and pulled into the parking lot, the light on his bike illuminating a body on the ground.

Holy shit. He parked and jogged over, only to slow as the person slowly lifted himself, groaning and holding his head. "Fucking whores."

"What did you do?" Dominick growled, feeling his fury bubble. His fists clenched as he stalked close enough to swing.

Thomas scrabbled back. "Don't you fucking touch me. I know what you are."

"You know shit, asshole. Where's Anika?"

"I don't know."

"And yet, here you are, in the parking lot of her work, looking like someone smashed your face in."

"It was that cunt. The one who sprang me from the hospital. Said she'd give me a thousand bucks to meet Anika."

The words ignited a prickle of unease. "And you, of course, sold her out. Who is she? What does this woman want?" Why did he have an icy fear that it had to do with him?

"Fuck you. I'm gonna find her first. Bitch fucking stiffed me for the money."

Dominick's phone vibrated. He ignored it. "What did she look like?"

His phone rang, and wouldn't stop ringing, annoying him enough that he answered with a snapped, "What?"

"Do you not check your phone?" It was Raymond. "You got a text from Anika. She's been kidnapped, dude."

Dominick didn't reply but checked his messages.

There it was, in bold text. But he didn't believe it. He hung up on Raymond and called Anika.

A man with a deep voice answered. "You must be the boyfriend."

"Where is she? What have you done with Anika?"

"Nothing. Yet. So, hurry up before that changes." *Click.*

Calling back didn't get a reply, and with a yell of frustration, Dominick flung the phone only to hear it start ringing.

Fuck. Fuck. Fuck!

He located the cracked device just as Raymond's call went to voicemail.

A text immediately followed. *Don't do anything stupid.*

Too late. Knowing Anika was in danger? All sense and reason went out the door.

He knew the cemetery he'd been told to go to. He

crouched low over the bike, gunning it hard to make it there fast. In his haste to park, the kickstand didn't engage properly, and the bike fell over. Stefan would beat him black and blue. He didn't care.

He had only one thought: Anika.

Nothing good could come from being in a cemetery at night. He still went through the gates and had to rely on starlight and a three-quarter moon to guide him.

Even with his military training, he missed them at first. Whoever had taken Anika knew to stand downwind and in a pocket of shadow deep enough back to keep them hidden until Dominick got to a certain point.

"That's far enough," a deep voice said, one that raised the hairs on his neck.

Dominick halted and clenched his fists. He sensed more than saw the figures that stepped out to surround him. He twitched, his skin itchy and tight. Uncomfortable.

"Who are you? Where's Anika?"

"Right here."

Anika suddenly emerged from behind a monument, coming to where he could see her. Eyes wide and frightened, mouth gagged, and hands bound in front of her.

His rage bubbled under the skin. "Release her."

"You don't get to make demands." The man

sounded amused as he stepped where he could also be seen. A tall and lean fellow with a dark shock of hair and a cruel twist to his lips.

"Who are you?" Dominick asked.

"You can call me Gwayne. And you are?"

"Nobody."

"Everyone has a name, friend. What's yours?"

When he would have remained silent, Anika made a sound as her hair was caught in a fist.

Dom trembled. "Dominick."

"Dominick, who?"

He didn't want to say. Didn't want his family brought into it.

But Anika…

"Hubbard."

"Was that really so hard? Now for the next one, *what* are you?"

"A dude."

"You're more than just a dude," Gwayne mocked.

"I'm ex-military, if that's what you're asking."

"Are you being deliberately obtuse? What do you think, gang?" Gwayne asked of his companions, reminding Dominick that he was alone against a group.

"Thomas Fitzpatrick, a man who had to get a hundred and fifty stitches, is claiming a panther attacked him." This came from the woman holding Anika.

"Thomas is a liar."

"Is he?" the woman asked. "Because he also claims he saw a naked man emerging from her apartment." She pointed to Anika. "And that the man turned into a cat."

"Obviously high. Seeing things that aren't there."

"Is he? Because I have to wonder. Your scent"—Gwayne angled his head—"is different than humans'."

The choice of words chilled him.

"Again, I'm going to ask, what are you? And before you lie, let me add incentive. Don't tell the truth, and she gets hurt." As if they were an act, the woman shoved Anika to her knees and drew her head back, exposing her throat.

Dominick snarled. He couldn't help it. "Don't touch her."

"You know how to keep her safe." The man didn't move, and yet the threat remained implicit.

He also obviously knew. The jig was up. The only thing Dominick could do at this point was bluff his way through and hope. "It's recently come to my attention that I'm an huanimorph."

"What the fuck is that?" exclaimed someone behind him.

"Would you understand if I said werepanther, instead?"

No shock or mockery appeared on the other

man's face. On the contrary, rather than laugh, Gwayne's gaze narrowed. "Shift and show me."

A snort escaped Dominick. "It's not that simple, buddy."

"Actually, it is. Niles, please demonstrate."

One of the fellows flanking him moved to his left and, to Dominick's disbelieving eyes, began to strip. But it was the fact that he changed from human flesh to wolf fur—in a contortion so fast and impossible— that had him gasping.

"Werewolf."

"We prefer the term Lycan."

"Lycan." He rolled the word around. "Is that what I am?"

Gwayne snorted. "Hardly. You are an oddity. A rumor that, until now, I didn't believe."

"Meaning what?"

"Lycans are the only true animal shifters."

Fake it to own it. He'd had a drill sergeant who used to bark that. "Guess again."

"Before I make my decision on your fate, shift."

"I can't."

The man didn't signal, and yet the woman tugged Anika's hair, causing her to cry out and the gag to loosen. "He needs catnip," she yelled.

Way to give up his kryptonite. Then again, he couldn't blame her.

It was just his luck that Gwayne didn't believe him. "You need *what* to shift?"

Dominick rolled his body as he admitted, "I only seem to go hairy when I eat catnip. Sniffing it just makes me horny and shit."

"Interesting."

"Meaning what? What did your buddy use to change shapes?" He pointed to the wolf sitting by Gwayne's side.

"A Lycan of strong blood needs nothing but willpower. The lessers require a full moon."

"You make it sound like there's lots of you."

"More than in your family."

That chilled him. "What do you know about my family?"

"Enough to say this conversation has been most enlightening." Gwayne snapped his fingers. "We'll be seeing you again soon."

"Why?"

"Because I am the Lycan Alpha of the Valley Pack. And you are an unaligned threat in my territory that now needs to be dealt with. Failure to do so won't end well."

With those final words, Gwayne left with his posse.

Dominick wasted no time running to Anika, snapping the ties binding her wrists and pulling the gag completely free. He then scooped her into his arms, buried his face in her neck, and breathed in her scent.

It couldn't calm the raging beast inside.

Which was why, once he got her back to her apartment, he knew he had to say goodbye.

22

THE BIKE RIDE WAS THRILLING AND QUIET, the roar of the engine and the whip of the wind making conversation impossible.

But once they got to her place, they couldn't avoid it.

"Are you okay?" he asked.

"Yeah. They didn't hurt me, really. More used me as a prop to scare you." Her nose wrinkled.

"I'm sorry." He sagged. "I had no idea I'd bring trouble down on you."

"You can't seriously be taking the blame for this. I'm pretty sure you didn't do it on purpose."

He shook his head. "It's been a weird twenty-four hours."

"Tell me about it."

"I shouldn't."

"I see." She could sense him closing himself off from her. Pulling some of his usual macho bullshit.

He exhaled. "I might be in danger. My whole family, actually. My brother Stefan thinks the lab that made us might still be after us."

She blinked. "Back up. What lab? Start from the beginning."

So, he did. Told her how they were made and smuggled out. How he never suspected he was different.

"You really have no clue what you're doing as the beast?"

He rolled his shoulders. "Nope. I'm just glad I didn't hurt you. Which is why I gotta stay away."

"You wouldn't hurt me." She knew it with a certainty she wouldn't argue.

"I'm dangerous."

"Only because it's new and you need to learn to control it."

"Yeah, by staying away from catnip."

"You said your brother has a handle on it. Why can't you? You're stronger than you know, Dom. You are, after all, a veteran."

"I see what you're doing," he grumbled.

"Trying to stop you from making a mistake. You are not breaking up with me, Dominick Hubbard. Not before I've at least tasted Thanksgiving dinner."

His lips twitched. "Actually, it would be cruel of

me to deprive you of Christmas Eve fondue, Christmas Day dinner, and Boxing Day leftover coma."

"I agree. Just like I've heard something about a mean Easter ham."

He ran his finger down the side of her face. "Staying with me could be dangerous. And I'm not talking about just me. Look at what happened tonight. My enemies kidnapped you."

"They also let us go." She cupped his cheeks. "Listen, I don't know where this is going yet. Other than a weird direction. But I want to stick to it for a bit. See if this thing between us can weather the fact that it's wild and kind of enjoyable."

"Only kind of?"

She grinned. "Maybe I need another demonstration of the perks."

"I don't deserve you, Anika." He huffed softly against her hair as he held her close.

"Just promise me I'll never see you licking your balls and coughing up hair."

"That isn't funny."

"If we don't laugh, what can we do?"

They could make love.

A quick and furious coupling that started with a kiss and ended with them naked, her clothes on the floor, her back against the wall, him sinking balls-deep into her.

She clawed his back and exhaled his name when she came.

She screamed when he later made love to her in bed.

She almost killed him, though, when he woke her early. Much too early, but she'd make an exception for sex.

"Come here," she purred, reaching for him.

Instead, he whipped back the covers. "Get up."

"Why?" she whined, reaching for the warmth. "It's my day off."

"Because we can't be late for breakfast."

"Pretty sure my box of cereal doesn't care what time it's being eaten." She'd splurged and gotten a name-brand version.

"Mom is making Belgian waffles with whipped cream, along with banana peanut butter crepes, peameal bacon, sausage, and..." He leaned close. "Her famous pumpkin spiced coffee, which she only makes one day a year."

"I'm sure she doesn't want an extra mouth to feed."

His brows shot up high. "You obviously don't know my mom well." His phone, with its cracked screen from its earlier flight, buzzed, and he gave it a quick glance before saying, "Maeve just texted. Says Mom heard you like eggs Benedict, so she's whipping up some fresh English muffins and prepping the sauce."

Her legs swung out of bed. "Is it too soon to say I love your mom?"

He grabbed her and swung her until she faced him. "Love my mom. Love me."

"Do I have to?"

She expected a cocky reply a la Dominick. Instead, he pressed his lips against her forehead and whispered, "I can only hope I'm good enough to be worthy of you."

As if there was any doubt. She couldn't have said when she fell in love, only that she knew for sure in that moment. But she didn't tell him until after breakfast when they lay in the backyard on a blanket, enjoying the autumn sun.

She had to unbutton her pants and groan. "I ate too much."

Who wouldn't love a man who patted her belly and said, "Wait until you see what we've got to eat for dinner. You'll look ready to give birth."

"Just make sure you leave room for dessert." And, yes, she winked as she said it.

Because she was in love with a man who could eat her—in all the best ways.

EPILOGUE

NANA GLANCED OVER HER FAMILY SEATED around the massive dining table, built by her boys while in high school. It had been repaired a few times since, as had the benches, but she was never happier than when it was full.

All but two of her children converged for dinner. Jessie, who'd been on a European tour for a few years now. Daeve, deployed and determined to give Nana gray hairs given his determination to show up his older brother with the number of missions he went on.

She had to remind herself that Dominick had made it back in one piece. And, even better, finally appeared to be settling in, thanks to Anika.

As they conversed over dinner, she thanked a god she didn't believe in for keeping her family safe and thanked all the spirits watching that she still had her children despite her secret being revealed.

Mostly. A few items she couldn't divulge still remained. She couldn't reveal them. Not yet. What if her fears never came to pass?

Then again, what if another of her children got an anonymous package?

Were they safe?

Thanksgiving dinner, the Canadian version being celebrated in October, involved lots of conversation about their origins. There was no point in keeping it secret from each other, especially once they discovered that Daphne had eavesdropped on the entire conversation.

The only one acting aloof with her was Stefan. Given how long he'd been hiding his striped secret, she could understand why.

They'd need to sit down and chat. Soon. But not tonight. Tonight was about too much food. Family. Love.

The knock at the door happened as they were about to have dessert. Pumpkin pie topped with whipped cream and drizzled with caramel. As she dished it, Stefan went to answer and returned with an envelope.

"What is that?" Odd getting mail, it being the holiday weekend and all.

"No idea, but it's addressed to the Hubbard

Family Clan," Stefan said with a frown as he turned it over in his hands.

"Maybe we won the lottery!" Daphne clapped her hands.

"Maybe, pipsqueak. Let's see what's inside."

They had to impatiently wait as Stefan tore open the envelope and pulled forth a gilded card.

He read it aloud.

"The Hubbard Family is to present itself to the Valley Pack on Halloween."

"Valley Pack? Those are the assholes who kidnapped Anika," Dominick blustered.

"Then they can go fuck themselves." Stefan lit the invitation on fire.

But he'd soon realize that it wasn't the kind of invitation that could be refused.

STEFAN WILL SOON DISCOVER THAT THE PRICE OF THEIR SURVIVAL WILL MEAN CURTAILING HIS OWN. FUR WILL FLY WHEN THIS TIGER MEETS A WOLF PRINCESS WHO DECIDES SHE WANTS HIM. THE PROBLEM BEING, SHE ISN'T THE ONLY ONE.

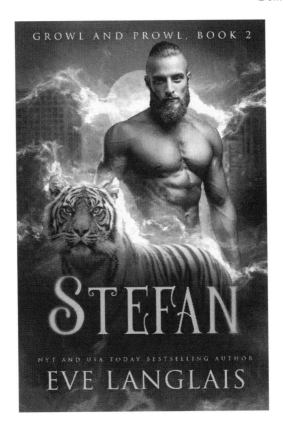

For more information or books (including many HOT shifters) see EveLanglais.com

Made in the USA
Columbia, SC
04 November 2021

48375260R00111